A FIONA MAHONEY MYSTERY

A VOCATION OF VIOLENCE

KERRIGAN BYRNE

OLIVERHEBERBOOKS

Chapter One

The Velvet Glove.

A den of iniquity draped in silk and lace.

It made me wish I'd donned some of the same for the occasion.

A place where London's wealthy and aristocratic came to shed their cloaks of respectability along with their overcoats.

I stepped inside, the heavy door thudding shut behind me, sealing off the chill of the February night. The air was thick with the scent of exhaled smoke and the musk of human desire. Gaslights cast a golden hue across the rich mahogany and gilt of the gaming tables, where fortunes were lost and won on the turn of a card.

"Good evening, Miss Mahoney," the burly doorman greeted me with a knowing leer. "I was told to expect you and to send you to the Shiloh room."

"Evening," I replied, my voice steady despite the tremor of anticipation that quivered through me.

His gaze lingered on my plain gray gown, but I refrained from wiping his smile away with a sharp retort. The courtesans of the Velvet Glove were swathed in less fabric but more finery than I would likely ever wear.

And that was all right with me.

Myriad mirrors reflected my image as I walked, a figure in an unassuming gown, designed to let me blend into the background. Yet I could not shake the feeling of being watched by unseen eyes.

In the corners, whispered deals conspired with seduction, while above, on balconies fit for royalty, women sparkled in jewels and little else, laughing with a timbre that landed hollow in my ear. The Velvet Glove caressed the wicked and washed away scruples and memories with glasses of amber liquid, sickly-sweet smoke, and white powder.

Here, secrets were currency, and I had come to spend a few of mine.

My hands, skilled in what some considered the macabre art of cleaning up after the dead, now clenched at the fabric of my skirt. I was no stranger to the remnants of violence, to the blood that spilled like a crimson confession upon the floor when a body gave up the ghost.

My best friend, Mary Kelly, hadn't been the first

murder victim I'd witnessed, but she'd been the first I'd cleaned up after.

Hers was what taught me how blood must be handled.

Making my way through the crowd of ten o'clock revelers, I chided myself. I needed to think of something other than murder. Tonight, I was at the Velvet Glove to commit a different transgression. But even as I sought distraction, *her* memory anchored me to a purpose darker than the indulgences surrounding me.

Vengeance.

It was what fueled me to rise every morning. What kept me like a fly buzzing around what the greatest city in the world shat onto the cobbles. What had me peering for monsters in every shadow.

For a single monster, really.

Jack the Ripper.

The villain who'd taken Mary from this world in the most gruesome way imaginable. The reprobate who sent me letters to taunt and terrify me, all while aiding in the resolution of more than two murders.

In his last missive, he'd demanded I remain "pure."

Which was why I'd come to the Velvet Glove.

To play with fire.

To disobey.

"Your first time is always the hardest." The remembered words cut through the din, though spoken only in my mind. Mary's young, singsong voice, a chime of the past, yet oddly fitting amidst this splendor. *"But if you have a*

bloke who knows the business, it can be quite...well, really lovely, actually."

Mary had been too young to know about intercourse that day when we put our heads together like silent sisters, giggling about newfound secrets and sins. I hadn't understood at the time, in our early teens, that her life had devolved into providing men liberties in exchange for survival. We were romantics, then.

Well, *I was*... I didn't think Mary was ever allowed the liberty of romanticism.

Not when it came to men.

I pushed the thought aside. This was no romantic endeavor for me. Not really. This was about power as much as pleasure. About taking control when it felt like I had none.

I decided when I took a lover and whom.

Not any of the Men Who Knew Better in my life.

And certainly not Jack.

"Miss Mahoney?" A young maid appeared at my side, her eyes downcast. "He awaits you upstairs."

"Thank you," I murmured, allowing her to lead me away from the glowing lights and noise, my heart a drumbeat against my ribs.

As we ascended, I couldn't help but thinking that the cleansing of blood was simpler than navigating the web of human emotions. Each step we took was a step closer to Jorah David Roth, to an encounter I had convinced myself was necessary—a lie I painted in shades of truth.

It was a choice, not a compulsion, a detail which mattered only to me.

Mary would understand, wouldn't she? I found myself seeking absolution from a ghost. She knew the weight of secrets, how they could chain you to a past that never ceased clawing its way into your present. She was forever going against what was expected of her.

It was one of the reasons I had loved her so dearly.

"Here we are, miss." The maid's voice pulled me back as she gestured to an ornate door. This threshold was unlike any crime scene I'd crossed before; yet, in some ways, it was exactly the same—a place where one left pieces of themselves behind.

Willingly or not.

I thanked the maid again, steeling my nerves as I reached for the knob. Behind this door was a man who could seduce with a glance, whose charm was as lethal as his criminal enterprise. I was about to barter with danger, and the price was a piece of my soul.

Or my body, at least.

It was the price that had been determined for me to grasp a semblance of power in a world determined to render me powerless.

The Shiloh room's door had yielded an inner sanctum that bore none of the Velvet Glove's garish splendor. Here, Jorah David Roth had crafted a haven of soft gold and ivory, a world away from the crimson drapes and heavy scents that marked the rest of his empire. As I let the door fall shut with a whisper, I realized that the true gamble wasn't at the tables—it was in the choices we made, the secrets we kept, and the desires we dared to chase.

Jorah David Roth, better known to the world as "the Hammer," had long made it known that he desired me. He'd made salacious offers I'd have slapped out of any other man's mouth.

One did not raise a hand to a man like Jorah without wishing for the grave.

Also, he'd promised me bliss. And though the Hammer was a man who ruled with an iron fist and unflinching ruthlessness, he did not trade in deceit.

At least, he'd always kept his word to me.

Even when those words had been threats.

I'd sent ahead a letter, sealed with wax and a courage I hadn't known I possessed.

His response had come promptly, penned in a hand that spoke of both precision and fever—a contradiction much like the man himself. And now, by the muted glow of gaslight chandeliers, I braced myself for a transaction that was all at once business, pleasure, and a surrender.

But it was more than that—there was an aching curiosity within me, a longing to taste life's darker fruits before they rotted on the vine.

Why him?

My empty bed had more than a few offers of fulfillment.

The words *handsome*, *charming*, and *skilled* felt like an understatement when sculpting Jorah's short list of virtues.

The rest were vices, and just as powerful a reason for me to turn to him for this act. He professed to being good at it, which many men did, but his reputation as a lover had already preceded him. He famously didn't partake of the women he sold, but he kept lovers. He beguiled women of the *ton* with his chameleonlike ability to blend with the lowest creatures of Whitechapel or the highest nobles at court. He was both rough and regal. Equally sordid and splendid.

This was no love match, mind, but a bargain struck where only flesh and whispers would be exchanged. A pact of ecstasy, devoid of promises except for pleasure.

However fleeting it might be.

The door clicked open again, and there stood Jorah, a study in controlled power. His dark hair, a contrast to the pale fabric of his impeccable shirt, caught the light as he moved with leonine grace. He surveyed me with hazel eyes that missed nothing, a slight smile playing about his lips that suggested secrets and sins interwoven.

"Miss Mahoney," he greeted me, the trace of a Russian accent coloring his words like a smear of ink on pristine paper. "You honor my humble establishment."

"Humble? I'd like to see your version of opulence." My tart reply came out steadier than I felt, but even so, the tremor of anticipation betrayed me.

Then annoyed me.

KERRIGAN BYRNE

Clumsy flirtation was all I could muster against his polished charm. Against anything, really. I was too practical to be a flirt, I think. Too graceless to fancy myself a temptress. Too freckled to be porcelain and too well fed to be willowy. I was at once too much and not enough for the likes of men such as him.

And he was one of the only men who hadn't said that to my face.

Another reason I found myself here tonight, I supposed. The Hammer could buy the most expensive woman in the world to share his bed.

And he wanted me for free.

"Tell me, Jorah," I began, cheeks warming under his gaze, "do you make all your guests feel as though they've stepped into a lion's den?"

"Only those brave enough to seek the lion," he replied in a velvet voice as dark as the lining of an expensive coffin.

"Then let's hope this lion doesn't bite," I said, an attempt at levity that escaped as sensual challenge.

"Ah, but Fiona," he murmured, tracing a long, elegant finger down the side of my face, "what if the lady does not yet know how much she would enjoy being devoured?" His touch sparked an involuntary shiver, one I couldn't disguise as he brought my skin to life.

I caught my breath as he leaned closer, his lips hovering over mine.

"I would never hurt you, Fiona," Jorah suggested, his

breath a warm caress against the late-winter chill lingering on my cheek. His hands found the small of my back, pulling me flush against his lean, hard body. "Unless you asked me to."

I couldn't imagine a world where I'd solicit additional pain.

At nine and twenty, I'd had enough to last lifetimes.

"Your breath smells of whiskey," he murmured, running a fingertip over the seam of my lips in a way that left a trail of sparks in its wake. "Are you afraid of me, Fiona?"

I didn't answer.

I was wise to fear him. There were secrets he would kill me for telling. Bodies I could uncover that would bring his tidy empire to its knees.

It was our impasse, I thought, that created this odd pocket of trust.

Once upon a time, when we were both desperate, he'd paid me to hide a body and clean up after. For many reasons, mostly that I'd mouths to feed and vengeance to reap, I had continued to do so upon occasion. The other reason was that anyone who decided to quit working for the Syndicate, the organization of which Jorah was a part, never lived long enough to seek other employment.

I hated him for tricking me into this place, but here we were a couple years later, still surviving.

Some would say...thriving.

"What changed your mind about us?" he crooned,

whispering covert kisses into my hairline, temples, and cheekbones. "About me?"

I couldn't bring myself to say any one of the million words that threw themselves at the vault of my lips, so I did something so uncharacteristic, it shocked both of us.

Lifting to my toes, I pressed my soft mouth to his hard one, hoping he could read physical subtext.

I couldn't say for certain if he understood me or not, but he was easily misdirected.

He deepened our kiss from a press of lips to a conflagration of need and nerve. For a few intense moments, all I could feel was the heat of his mouth against mine and the pressure of his hands on my back.

I was grateful for the kiss, for its ability to silence my thoughts and bring me to the present moment. As the intensity of our kiss grew, my doubts and reservations began to melt away. Jorah's expert touch awakened a hunger within me, a craving for something forbidden yet alluring. In that moment, I gave in to the heat that had smoldered between us for longer than a year now.

Even in the midst of our intoxicating embrace, my mind couldn't help but wander to the reason I had sought him out once again. The secrets I had kept for him, the bodies I had buried—they were a constant reminder of the darkness that surrounded us both. I had become entangled in his world, unable to escape it.

Was this the true reason for my surrender?

As my blood melted to honey beneath his caresses,

the answer became irrelevant. His fingers deftly worked the buttons of my blouse, which surrendered to him more readily than to myself or any maid.

I was teetering on the edge of reason and ruin when an odd knock sounded at the door, tearing us apart like a cold gust of wind snuffing out a flame.

The knock at the door twisted into a peculiar rhythm, a staccato that seemed out of place amidst the Velvet Glove's usual symphony of sin.

Ripping his mouth from mine, Jorah tossed a rebuke over his shoulder at the door. "Sod off!"

The knock repeated without hesitation. The same odd, broken rhythm as before.

The muscles of his back that'd become molten beneath my questing hands turned to steel again. "I said I was not to be disturbed!" he roared.

A dratted third time and I recognized the increasingly aggressive knock as some sort of code.

Jorah muttered something fierce in a foreign language, a frown creasing his brow. "Forgive me, Fiona. It seems this pleasure must wait its turn."

"Oh—o-of course," I replied.

I was barely allowed the time to hastily clutch my shawl from the back of a chair to cover the expanse of my decolletage above my exposed corset. The interruption stung, a reminder that in this house, secrets were currency and time was a luxury few could afford.

Jorah's expression soured from dangerous to

murderous as he yanked open the door. "Enter," he commanded, his voice laced with annoyance.

My rushing blood stilled at the sight of Aramis Night Horse.

In the Syndicate, if Jorah was the Hammer, then Night Horse was known as "the Blade."

The juxtaposition of his presence against the Shiloh room's genteel decor was stark. He was all hard angles and silent power, his black eyes inscrutable beneath the fall of his long hair the color of midnight. His features bore the stoic beauty of his Blackfoot heritage, and there was an enigmatic tilt to his lips, suggesting secrets even Jorah wasn't privy to.

I knew the fires that forged him into the assassin that he was.

They'd burned me, too.

"Roth." His tone held no deference, though his words did. "They've arrived early."

I sensed rather than saw the moment Night Horse noticed me. By the time my light green gaze collided with his dark one, I'd almost missed the displeasure flickering across his face.

There was history there, too, a story written in the briefest of glances between us—a memory of a kiss bought and paid for that now hung heavy in the air.

Yet, just as quickly, his gaze slid from mine, dismissing the past as if it were weightless and worthless.

"Do I not pay a queen's ransom to keep people

entertained?" Jorah asked, his hand lingering at my waist, possessive even in his irritation. "No one can manage to distract them until the festivities begin?"

Festivities? Whatever arousal had bloomed beneath his touch died on that word.

Jorah had planned to take my virginity, and then... what? Attend a party?

I swallowed the next thought, though it tasted like acid in my throat.

What had I expected?

At the moment I hadn't the answer for myself...but apparently I'd assumed we'd make a night of it.

"The Dublin Destroyer, he's—insisting on an audience." Dark eyes found me again before flicking away. A muscle worked beneath his smooth jaw. "Before midnight."

Jorah cursed under his breath, his fingers absently toying at my lower back as he pinched the bridge of his nose with his other hand. "Give us a moment, Night Horse."

But it was too late.

The door burst open as if those spilling past it had overflowed a crowded room rather than an empty hallway. Two men and two women strutted into the Shiloh room with the fanfare of a circus troupe—each one a character so vibrant they seemed to bleed color into the muted tones of the office.

One might have knocked me over with a feather for all their cheek.

Jorah had killed men for less. This was his sanctuary of solitude, as he had a separate office from which he conducted his more...people-facing business.

Only his inner circle ever ventured here.

And me, once, when I was brought here to convalesce after a rather brutal attack in the streets.

The first through the door glittered like a star plucked from the night sky, her gaze sweeping the room with the confidence of a queen surveying her court. She shimmered with an incandescent beauty that couldn't be diminished were she wrapped in sack cloth and ashes.

She wasn't. Her siren-scarlet gown cost more than my stately rowhouse on Tite Street, I was certain.

A mousy girl with dark gold curls hovered near her elbow, her admiration for the lovely woman as palpable as the heat from a fire.

They were followed by a garden rake of a man, whose eyes darted about with calculating shrewdness, taking in more than he would ever let on.

"Forgive the intrusion, Mr. Roth," boomed a deep Irish brogue, thick and unapologetic. "We've urgent business that couldn't wait until—"

My. God.

I stood frozen, a blush creeping up my neck as I clumsily pulled the shawl closer, attempting to completely conceal the indecency of my partial undress.

But, as all eyes turned to me, every breath, every heartbeat, was suspended in the shock of revelation.

The room fell into a charged silence as the final player in this unexpected gathering moved closer to me, his heavy steps resounding against the plush carpets.

I swallowed hard, the words I intended to speak lodging in my throat, strangled by memories and emotions I hadn't realized still clung to me like ivy to ancient stone.

His whispered name hung in the air, a ghostly chord struck upon the strings of our shared history, leaving the room in silent anticipation of what secrets lurked beneath the surface.

"Fi?" It escaped him like a prayer. One of many we'd been forced to say together upon a holy mass.

"No... I... I don't believe it's you! It's impossible," I exclaimed, taking two steps back in disbelief.

His laugh was deep and bittersweet.

"If I've learned one thing, Fiona Mahoney, it's that the past will find us in the most unexpected places."

Chapter Two

The chill of the Shiloh room did naught to cool the fire that danced in Darcy O'Dowd's eyes, nor the sudden blaze it kindled within my own.

There he stood—"the Dublin Destroyer"—as if plucked from the girlhood memories I'd thought long interred with the rest of my past in Limerick, Ireland. A home I'd not seen in almost five years.

Our gazes latched on to each other, a silent communication thrumming between us, fraught with disbelief and the weight of so many years spent apart.

"Good heavens." A silken and melodious voice cut through the moment like a blade, the lovely woman immediately commanding attention. Her beauty was not just observed but felt, like an enchantment that left one spellbound. Her gown clung to her curves in a shameless embrace, the color of blood and studded with stars, her golden hair coiffed high but for a few ringlets cascading over her shoulder.

"Forgive me," she announced to the room at large, "my entrance seems to have interrupted...something quite intimate?" Her gaze swept between Jorah, Darcy, and me, her lips curved in the smile of a Cheshire cat as she extended her hand with regal grace to accept a kiss on the proverbial ring.

From whom, I couldn't tell.

Not me, surely.

I was still trying to collect my wits, first lost to Jorah's kiss, then kicked under the rug by Night Horse's arrival, now vanquished by the ghosts of the past.

The last thing I needed was a reminder that I'd been caught nearly naked with a notorious criminal to make my heart leap from its home in my chest to the acid in my belly.

"Viv!" Darcy's brogue, rich and warm, was a stark contrast to the brisk London air that had seeped into the bones of the place. He curled a braw arm around her barely there waist, even as his eyes never left me. "You'll never believe this, me pet. You remember me blatherin' on about me old mates when we were lads in Limerick? The two most troublemaking twins south of the River Shannon, Finn and Flynn Mahoney—not even poor Aidan could keep us all in line." If he was thrown by his companion's astute observation of just what they'd interrupted between Jorah and me, he gave zero indication. "This was their wee little sister, Fiona Mahoney!"

Was.

Though I tried to summon a smile, my guts twisted at the mention of my brothers.

Of Aidan. He had been many things to me. My first love. My fiancé. My soldier on a distant shore.

My greatest disappointment.

One of my worst recent memories.

Closing off the ill-timed use of that name and the emotions it evoked, I forced myself to find words.

"Charmed," I managed, my voice nearly catching in my throat as I tore my gaze from Darcy to address the alluring intruder that was quite obviously his...paramour? Fiancée? Friend? Spouse?

My cheeks flushed with heat, more embarrassment, now, than arousal.

"Likewise," she replied, her smile as effervescent as champagne bubbles. Surprisingly, she seemed not to care about the undercurrents she'd waded into, her whiskey eyes twinkling with mischief.

"From Limerick, you say?" Vivienne arched a brow, her interest piqued as she looked back toward Darcy. "Well, Miss Mahoney, is it? Allow me to do what this thickheaded cretin never learned the manners to, and introduce myself." She elbowed past Darcy, who stepped aside with an affable gesture so she and I could shake hands. "I happen to be Vivienne Bloomfield-Smythe of the Dorset Smythes. What brings you to this sordid corner of London?"

"Business," I responded, reaching out from beneath the shawl to awkwardly press her hand and perform the ghost of a curtsy.

I could scarcely fathom the turn of fate that had brought Darcy, someone so integral to my childhood, here to the Shiloh room. The very room where secrets whispered along the walls and shadows held their breath.

It was no place for past lives to resurrect, nor for fond memories to find new life.

But there he was.

Darcy O'Dowd... And with him, the ghost of innocence that I'd long since buried beneath mossy stones stained with the blood of everyone I ever loved.

"Business?" Vivienne echoed, her lips curling around the word as though it were a delectable secret. "How very cryptic of you, Miss Mahoney. Am I to assume, Darcy darling, that she is employed here at the Velvet Glove?" She did a not-so-surreptitious sweep of my person, noting my more uniform attire and chignon arranged by my own hand rather than that of a lady's maid.

"Perhaps," Darcy agreed, though it was clear his mind was still half entangled in the web of our unexpected reunion. He blinked several times, his brow furrowing beneath russet hair, slicked back with pomade, shades darker than his impressive ginger mustache. "I hear from back home that you followed poor Mary out here to do the—uh—the business. I says to me manager, Georgie here, I says, 'Pray to St. Brigid that it i'nn't so! Pretty little Fiona Mahoney was fed to the London wolves after life already done her so dirty.' Didn't I say that, old boy? When we heard what happened to Mary?"

The room, a tapestry of shocked shadows, seemed suddenly to shrink as George Tunstall made himself known. Unlike the vibrant display that Vivienne Bloomfield-Smythe had offered upon her arrival, Tunstall's presence cast a pall over the Shiloh room, his dour countenance like a storm cloud on an otherwise unblemished horizon. His eyes, cold chips of flint, surveyed the assembly with an air of distaste, as if he could barely tolerate the company he was forced to keep.

"Indeed," he said, though his waspish voice held none of the warmth required by such a validation.

"Right!" Darcy said. "As my girl here has pointed out, I'm shite at introductions."

"Your girl?" I couldn't help but beam at the beauty beside him. "Are you engaged to Miss Bloomfield-Smythe, Darcy? Good on you for finding such a gem."

It was Vivienne's high, almost hysterical laugh that threw me off my axis once again, especially when she gripped my wrist as if she needed my help to process the lunacy of my question. "Lord but you're charming, Fiona—I can call you Fiona, can I not? The answer to your question is categorically *not*. Two marriages were enough for me, though you'd have to be Goliath to tear me away from this brute. I just adore every little thing about him." She nuzzled her nose against Darcy's, and I couldn't help but rub at a hollow pang in my chest.

He shot me a sheepish look from beneath a blush as he rubbed at a rouge stain on his cheek from her kiss. "I hope that doesn't shock you, Fi, me living in sin and all."

I didn't even know if I was capable of being shocked anymore. Not in the way he meant.

"I'm in no position to judge," I murmured, flicking a look at Jorah from beneath lowered lashes.

Darcy's toothy gold grin reminded me so much of the past that it hurt to breathe for a moment. "Good on us both, eh?" He nodded toward Jorah. "Two dowdy Catholics from a mud bog ending up with two—"

"You aren't finished with your introductions, Darcy," Vivienne cut in, her fingers on his coat turning into talons.

Darcy shook himself and glanced back over his shoulder to the storm cloud in the corner lurking like a ghoul. "This is George Tunstall, my brilliant manager and shadow."

We nodded to each other, though he made no move to take my hand, and I had no need to offer it.

"And this is?" I asked, smiling at the sprite of a girl trying to meld with Vivienne's skirts. She couldn't be more than sixteen, though her eyes already bore the shadows poverty benighted upon the young.

Vivienne flapped her gloved hand over the girl as if to erase her like pungent smoke. "Oh, that's just Claudia, my maid. She'll be invisible again when we're settled in our rooms."

Not to me, she wouldn't. "It's nice to meet you, Claudia."

She lifted her eyes to Vivienne and had to receive a nod of permission before returning the sentiment.

"It seems we've interrupted some sort of...affair and should excuse ourselves so they might...reclaim their dignity." Tunstall sniffed toward the shawl and bodice that would be gaping open if I'd not been clasping them both closed.

At least I thought he said "sort of." It might have been "sordid," as he was obviously the kind of man who didn't shrink from giving offense.

I wanted to tell him where he could shove his dignity, and might have done so if I weren't suddenly desperate for everyone to do exactly what he suggested and give us the room so I could fix myself.

"George, your disposition lights up a room, as per usual," Vivienne quipped, her words laced with a wry irony that did not go unnoticed by the manager.

"Mr. O'Dowd," Tunstall replied tersely, nodding with a formality that belied their close professional relationship. "Should we not step into the vestibule and—"

"Fi, I just can't believe it's really you." The timbre of Darcy's voice stroked the air, rich and smooth as aged whiskey as he rushed to me, crushing me to him in an exuberant embrace, not seeming to notice my arms caught between us.

He held me by the shoulders away from him. "Let me get a look at you, girl—you grew up a fine beauty, and that's a fact. Poor Flynn and me were keeping our knuckles sharp in case any of the lads got fresh with you, and now look at me." He released my shoulders so he could throw a few tiny faux punches into the air between us. "Sharper than the coral that tore up me da's fishing net, eh?"

Despite myself, despite the extra pair of eyes on us, I found myself swept away in his exuberance like we all did back home. Darcy O'Dowd had lost none of his impish boyhood vitality, even though he'd quite obviously lost a few teeth to his profession and replaced his front fang with one of gold.

He often stood shorter than other men in his presence, but somehow managed to seem more immense. The gaslight played upon his visage, throwing into relief the chiseled jawline and the set of broad shoulders honed through a boyhood of hard labor and, apparently now, countless battles in the ring. A mane of ruddy hair used to fall carelessly across his brow, but the hairline was fading further from where I remembered.

He still had those piercing eyes that danced with mirth and pulled unlikely women of Vivienne's ilk to his side. She was obviously besotted with him, even though she stood taller in her heeled slippers.

"I'm just so pleased for you, Darcy," I managed,

feeling every bit the girl who once roamed the green hills of Limerick with him and my brothers. "You set out to follow your dream and find your fortune, and you're the only one of us who did."

The light in his eyes dimmed. "Aye, well..." He finally seemed to notice the situation over the space between us charged with memories only we shared. "Ye've grown."

"More than you, it seems," I teased, the corner of my mouth lifting despite the heaviness in my heart. There was comfort in the familiar filial jibe, a momentary respite from the suffocating tension of my current life.

"Ah, but it's not height that measures the worth of a man, Fi, but the size of his fight." His laughter, deep and contagious, filled the room, in stark contrast to Tunstall's simmering displeasure and Jorah's uncharacteristic silence.

"Or woman," I corrected him, with a cheeky smirk.

"Or woman," he agreed, the acknowledgment spoken like a shared secret.

We stood there, two souls momentarily lost in a past that seemed both a lifetime ago and as immediate as the beating of our hearts. The warmth of our reunion flickered like a candle in the room, threatened by the encroaching chill of truths yet to be spoken.

"Never thought I'd find you in a place like this." A silence fell upon the Shiloh room, thick and expectant, as Darcy asked me questions with his eyes. Shadows played across his features, etching out the boy I once knew in the lines of the man before me.

Jorah finally stepped forward, resting his hand at my elbow with surprising circumspection. "Fiona is employed by me from time to time, but not in the capacity you assume. She is the proprietress of her own business, and our paths often cross...professionally."

Darcy's eyebrows lifted in astonished speculation. "I'll be beggared! What business are you about these days, Fi?"

"I'm a crime scene cleaning specialist."

His mouth dropped open. "Learned from your da, I expect."

The bottom emptied out of my stomach, and I had to bite my tongue to keep from revealing something I didn't want to. Jorah, Night Horse, and all the men like them who would use information as a weapon knew very little about me or my past.

As little as I could manage.

For the past was a place I rarely visited. It held nothing for me but pain.

"Oh God, Fi, your family...," Darcy began, his eyes reflecting a sorrow that matched the dark waters of the Thames at midnight.

"Is in the past," I cut in quickly, a sharpness in my tone that belied my usual calm. The ache for them was a constant companion, an old wound that refused to heal. "Let's keep our ghosts locked back there tonight, shall we?"

"Of course, Fiona," he acquiesced, his smile returning, though it did not reach his eyes.

Before I could breathe again, Vivienne Bloomfield-Smythe sashayed into our shared remembrance, her presence a sudden burst of color against the room's muted hues. She was an opulent bloom amongst wilting petals, her every movement deliberate and captivating.

"Darlings, forgive my intrusion of your heart-melting nostalgia," she cooed, her voice a melody that danced through the air with practiced grace. Her eyes, bright and unyielding, landed on me. "But I can't let another moment go by before demanding if that is what you planned to wear to the Midnight Bacchanalia? I mean, the shawl is lovely, and the—we'll call it a frock, dear—is well made, but woefully dreary for such an occasion as Darcy's exhibition and my London debut, if you don't mind my saying so!"

I did mind her saying so but was brought up too well to mention so.

Instead, a blush stained my cheeks, an unwelcome guest revealing emotion I was otherwise good at hiding. "I'm—I had no plans to attend an event tonight, Miss Bloomfield-Smythe, bacchanalia or otherwise." I left out that I hadn't been aware of such a fete, let alone invited.

"Just swept by for a bit of slap 'n' tickle with our Mr. Roth?" Vivienne purred, her gaze flickering between Jorah and me with unabashed curiosity. "You have the look of a woman who has just tasted the forbidden fruit."

Our Mr. Roth? I lifted an eyebrow at Vivienne. Was she implying what I thought she was implying?

"Vivienne!" Jorah chided gently, but not before a knowing smirk had crept onto his face.

"Everyone knows to call me Viv," she insisted, looping her arm through mine with the familiarity of a longtime confidante. "And do promise you'll share with me the details later. For inspiration, you understand."

I understood next to nothing.

"Perhaps," I said noncommittally, my thoughts already racing ahead. The weight of my shawl was suddenly oppressive, heavy with implications and the scent of clandestine affairs. I felt exposed under the scrutiny of the company, my secrets threadbare beneath the guise of finery.

Apparently having had enough, Jorah stepped between us all. "You've arrived two hours early to an event for which you planned to be an hour or two late should you want to make an entrance. Am I to understand there is a problem?" Even when speaking like a gentleman, Jorah could sound as ominous as an undertaker.

Lamplight danced like phantoms across the Shiloh room, glinting off the sheen of sweat on Darcy's brow. He leaned forward, his voice a low growl brimming with antipathy. "Georgie and me, we checked in at the warehouse to see how preparations are coming along, and we met an inspector keen on revoking the permits. I told him this exhibition fight is likely to be a spectacle London hasn't seen since Her Majesty's Golden Jubilee."

"I imagine that went over well," Jorah muttered.

Darcy's eyes darkened, but he shrugged. "Must have been a fan of t'other local fella I'm meeting in the ring."

"Bastard said he'd take the word of the devil himself over that of an Irishman. I told him we'd send him to the devil to ask." Tunstall startled everyone by vehemently stating the fact in his perfect, highborn British tongue. Not a pleasant fellow, but he did seem to take the right side of the Irish War.

At least in my view.

Jorah, his eyes reflecting the gleam of a predator in the half-light, nodded with a knowing smirk. "Every now and again a new hire at some bureaucratic office will get a wild hair before his peers let him know how these things work in my city. If there is a permit issue, I'm certain it will be fixed before it even reaches my ears. That is how my organization is run, Mr. O'Dowd. But I will find out before the party tonight, so you may join the revelry with an unburdened mind."

"I believe it," Darcy replied, his fists clenching as if he could already feel the crush of the crowd, the roar of the masses. "Me mind is never burdened with much, but that's why me fists make me money. This bout will give me enough to retire on and grow old. Every penny wagered will sing a siren's song to the chance takers and rabble-rousers of this city." He clapped his palms and danced a little celebratory jig with a barely willing Vivienne.

My heart should have been racing at the talk of fights and fortunes, but it sat heavy in my chest, an anchor dragging me down into the dark depths of disappointment.

I had envisioned an evening tangled in bedsheets with Jorah...

And he'd scheduled deflowering me for the two hours before a party?

"What could you possibly have to do more entertaining than a Midnight Bacchanalia with dear Darcy and I as the guests of honor? Especially after such a sweet reuniting," Vivienne said, her voice a silken caress that seemed to make the very air around us shiver with delight. "The Velvet Glove has promised an affair more decadent than Saturnalia itself. I don't think Darcy nor I would be able to enjoy it if you weren't there."

I doubted that very much as I searched my muddled mind for an excuse.

"Perhaps another time? As you've said, I'm not—er —dressed for the occasion." My voice cracked as I spoke, betraying my dismay. The words were a cold splash of reality against the warm embers of my recent almost-tryst.

"Indeed," Jorah said, turning his gaze upon me. His eyes bored into mine, enigmatic and deep as an abyss. "I did promise a celebration befitting a champion. You *must* attend, Fiona."

"Must I?" It was meant to be a defiance, a reclamation of the night I had planned, but it emerged as little more than a whisper lost amid the intrigue.

"Of course." Darcy's insistence was earnestly hopeful, brooking no argument. "After all, who better to grace the occasion than the girl I loved like me own sister? I can think of nothing happier."

A part of me yearned to be there. The part that was friends with a flighty Mary Kelly upon a day. I wanted to don a ball gown and waltz until dawn drove me home.

But I didn't live a life like that. Not like these people.

Jorah lowered his head until his lips caressed my ear, his touch scorching against my skin. "Forgive the intrusion, Fiona, but once tonight's festivities are well underway, we can disappear. And my bed and body will be all yours."

The promise, whispered with the intimacy of a secret pact, should have soothed the sting of rejection, yet it only served to deepen the wound. For it was not the promise of what was to come that pained me, but the stark realization of what would not be—a quiet night where the ghosts of my past and the specter of Jack the Ripper could be forgotten, if only for a few hours.

"Then it is settled," Vivienne declared, her smile bright as she surveyed our little gathering, blind to the shadows creeping at the edges of my consciousness.

"Settled," I echoed, my voice hollow as I forced a smile to match hers.

"You'll wear one of my evening gowns, of course." Her laughter was like the tinkling of fine crystal, and it chafed against my already frayed nerves. I glanced down at the simple garment that covered my shoulders—a far cry from the silken finery draped over her lithe form.

"I appreciate your generosity, but I've no need for —" My protest faltered, for she had already turned, summoning the young maid, who materialized as if conjured by the very air of expectation that Vivienne exuded.

"Claudia, be a dear and fetch the emerald satin from my latest collection. The one with the lace overlay. Our Miss Mahoney here will outshine the moon itself," she instructed the girl, her voice threaded with a command that left no room for dissent.

The doe-eyed maid curtsied and hastened away, leaving me to reckon with this unforeseen turn of events. A gown. A party. A night where the façade of normalcy would be as flimsy as the silk I was to be swathed in.

"Miss Bloomfield-Smythe, I fear I am ill-suited for such revelry," I murmured, my gaze dropping to my worn hands—hands that knew more of blood and grime than ballrooms and gaiety.

"I insist you call me Viv." Vivienne's hand fluttered to rest upon my arm, her touch featherlight yet somehow anchoring. "Consider it a boon from me to you. After all, we women must support each other in this world dominated by men and their brutish pursuits."

The weight of her gesture pressed upon me, the unspoken obligation wrapping around my ribs like the laces of a corset, tightening with each breath. The rich hue of her gown gleamed in the lamplight, a stark contrast to the dark shadows that seemed to cling to my soul.

I was supposed to spend the night either making love to Jorah or hunting Jack.

Not...this.

I would love the opportunity to connect with Darcy, though a party in his honor was the last place in which we could swim in the deep lake of our nostalgia together.

"Will you not seize the chance to cast aside your shadows, even if only for an evening?" Jorah's voice, soft and coaxing, drew me back from the precipice of my thoughts.

I stood there, torn between the desire to flee into the anonymity of the night and the yearning to step into the light, however briefly. Could I dare to embrace the respite offered, or would the pretense simply serve to underscore the grim reality of my existence?

"Very well, Miss—er, Viv," I said at last, a sense of resignation settling over me like a shroud. "I am more than honored to accept your generous offer."

"Exquisite," she breathed, satisfaction curling her

lips, and I wondered if this was a scene she had orchestrated—a play in which I had unwittingly been cast as the reluctant ingenue.

With Vivienne's offer hanging in the air like the heady aroma of night-blooming jasmine, I felt an invisible tether pulling me toward a destiny I was not sure I wanted to meet.

"I think you will enjoy yourself," Jorah said, his voice smooth as silk yet heavy with unspoken promises. "It shall be a night to remember."

"You'll have the first dance," Darcy threw in by way of sweetening the pot. "The second dance," he amended after Vivienne stomped on his toe.

I offered them a tight smile, my fingers absently tracing the intricate needlework of the shawl that had drawn Vivienne's teasing compliment earlier. The fabric seemed to whisper secrets of its own, secrets that could dance seductively on the edge of revelation in the glow of the upcoming festivities.

"I can't see how I could refuse," I said with a smile summoned from Lord-knows-where.

Finally, I glanced toward Night Horse, who remained conspicuously silent, his somber gaze fixed upon a point somewhere beyond the room's gilded confines. His lethal presence served as a stark reminder that not all that glittered was gold, and not all revelries ended when the music stopped.

He was a part of the night, especially at the Velvet Glove.

"Shall I see you all settled, then, and Fiona can dress in your rooms, Viv?" Jorah asked, his eyes never leaving mine.

"You plucked the thought from my mind," she replied, tucking her arm into Darcy's as Jorah led the way.

I fell in line behind Vivienne's bustle, minding the length of her train as we climbed the gilded stairs, feeling the weight of my choice settle upon my shoulders like a mantle. As they all began to discuss the logistics of the evening, I paused on a stair midway up, allowing myself the luxury of apprehension.

"You look like you're climbing to the gallows," Night Horse said from alarmingly close behind me. Closing the space between us, his warmth momentarily dispelling the chill of foreboding that didn't belong to a night such as this.

I fought the urge to explain my presence in Jorah's room.

In his arms.

But then I firmly reminded myself that Night Horse liked to make me uncomfortable on purpose because the blighter knew that I was chatty when nervous. Probably more than anyone. Because I was never *not* nervous in his presence.

"I hadn't prepared for society," I murmured over my shoulder. He seemed to understand that there were some people who could only stand the company of others for a finite amount of time.

It was something we had in common, I thought.

"Maybe tonight, instead of chasing death, Fiona Mahoney finally *lives*," he whispered, leaning close enough that I could feel his breath against my ear.

His words, meant to comfort, felt more like a sentence. And as the clock struck the hour, signaling the inexorable march toward midnight, I knew there would be no turning back.

"Tonight," I echoed, my resolve hardening. "Tonight, I live."

I'd no idea that in order for me to do so, someone would have to die.

Chapter Three

I found it easiest to disappear in a room full of people.

But I learned Vivienne Bloomfield-Smythe didn't own a dress capable of blending in.

The emerald gown she'd selected suited my complexion moderately well, and Vivienne had said it lit my hair like a sunset. There hadn't been the time to do much else with my hair, but she had her maid, Claudia, adorn the simple chignon with glittering glass pins that twinkled like stars.

"Come now, Claudia, do try to keep up." Vivienne's tone, once smooth as the finest claret, now cut through the hallway with a sharpness bordering on shrill. "Once you've arranged my train for my ovation, I need you to slink to the table and make certain I'm not seated next to anyone dreary, unattractive, or boorish."

"Yes, mistress." Claudia scuttled behind us as if tethered to the train that sashayed with each of Vivienne's steps.

The bon vivant leaned over to murmur in my ear, "That will keep the simple creature out of sight for a while. She does fray my nerves with her hovering before long."

I directed a frown at her, wondering why I felt the need to be careful with my words in her company.

Vivienne was a vision; not even the candlelight could compete with the incandescence of her beauty. It wasn't just her looks that made her the cynosure of all eyes, but the dangerous glimmer of something untamed in her gaze. If I was to be kind, I'd say it was a wildness... but if I were honest, it spoke of a hint of malice beneath the charm.

"Vivienne, you know she can't rearrange a place sett —" I began, but Vivienne cut me off with a graceful wave of her hand, her bracelets chiming like the bells of a distant church.

"Really, Fiona, this is the Velvet Glove. I doubt Jorah will even notice, let alone mind."

"In that case"—I glanced over my shoulder— "shouldn't Claudia be allowed to attend?"

Vivienne's lips curled into a smile that did not quite meet her eyes. "This night is for the upper echelons of society, not for those who lurk in the shadows of their betters."

"I don't consider anyone here any better than

Claudia or I." I could feel my Irish temper rising, readying for a verbal evisceration of someone who wouldn't deem me capable of licking her boots had I not been in the arms of a wealthy, powerful man when she'd interrupted what had promised to be a pleasant evening.

I watched as Claudia's expression crumpled, her devotion to Vivienne a fragile thing, too easily bruised. I knew that look, the pain of loyalty unappreciated, but there was also something else—a flicker of darkness that skittered across her features and vanished just as quickly.

Couldn't say I blamed her.

As effervescent and generous as Vivienne had been in the short hours I'd known her, I'd learned she'd a vicious wit and an incapacity to care much for anything beyond her own whims.

"Yes, miss," Claudia replied, her voice barely above a whisper as she retreated deeper into the curl of her shoulders.

I watched Claudia go, the unease coiling tighter in my gut. I knew what it was to be dismissed, to be seen as less than in the eyes of those who believed their birthright elevated them above common decency. But tonight, I pushed away the pity that threatened to rise, lest I ruin an old friend's special evening.

I scanned the crowd, looking for Darcy.

"Chin up, Fiona," Vivienne purred, looping her arm through mine. "The night is young, and there are secrets here ripe for the plucking—if one knows where to look."

Before I could reply, she burst from the hallway to the top of the grand staircase, her arms lifted like the pope addressing Vatican Square from his balcony.

The room erupted in applause, which she accepted graciously as her due.

I hovered in the shadow of the hall until she'd descended a few stairs to meet the first push of people awaiting the grace of her attentions. Only when no one watched the crest of the stairs did I step into the open space.

The air was thick with the scent of roses, tobacco smoke, and desire, a heady mixture that clung to the insides of my lungs like a whispered confession. The Velvet Glove Midnight Bacchanalia unfurled before me in a riot of silk and sensual delight, as if I had stepped into one of Hieronymus Bosch's fevered visions wrought into splendid reality. The ballroom was awash with the glow of a hundred candles, their flames casting shadows that danced lasciviously against walls draped with velvet so deep and red it might have been wrung from the heart of an unrepentant devil.

I felt a queer thrill at the decadence. I stood a voyeur ensnared by the spectacle of high society at its most debauched. Below me, ladies swathed in layers of lace and jewels twirled with men whose eyes betrayed more hunger than could ever be satisfied by a feast laid out on silver platters.

Despite the closeness of so many bodies, a shiver poured acid down my spine, a reminder that amid the splendor, danger often wore the most beguiling of masks.

I found Jorah holding court by a fireplace as tall as himself, resplendent enough for an audience with the queen. He lifted a hand to the nape of his neck before his eyes lifted from the gathered gentlemen to find mine.

He could sense when he was watched, as well.

We made dark, silent promises to each other as he gave me more compliments with his gaze than any kind word uttered about my gown.

Darcy broke from the crowd, looking rough-and-tumble despite the white-tie finery. He mounted the stairs to press champagne to Vivienne's hand and conducted her down to the dance floor, beside which a chamber orchestra poised to play.

Her champagne disappeared in a few sips before they opened the revelry with their own dance.

Though there was an obvious affection between the two, they didn't dance at all well together. Untrue to his Irish heritage, Darcy had never been a gifted dancer, but I didn't remember him being such a clod-foot.

True to his word, however, he found me for the second dance, and by the time we took our places, the floor filled quickly with other couples.

He apologized through a twitching mustache for any injuries I was about to sustain, but he managed to only step on my toe twice. "It's unfortunate that I can remember the complicated steps in the ring, but take me out of those confines and I might as well have turnips for toes."

"You're doing splendidly," I lied, just happy to be in his presence for the moment.

Night Horse had been right—I needed a night like this.

I needed to learn how to live.

Once the waltz ended, Darcy and I drifted to where Vivienne shimmered like a dark blood sea under a moonlit sky, her laughter now dancing upon the heavy air.

I watched in grim fascination as her charm, once wielded with precision, now frayed at the edges, unraveling with every sip of amber-gold liquid. How she'd already become inebriated after we'd only left her for one dance was bewildering to me. Twice in her dressing room and once in the hall, I'd seen her sniff a secretive powder concealed within the folds of her delicate handkerchief, and I now realized the substance wasn't at all benign.

"Darling!" Vivienne cooed at Darcy a touch too loudly as we approached. "Meet Baron Morton and his... daughter?" She gestured to an elderly gentleman whose monocle quivered where he'd trapped it over his eye. A petite, lovely, dark-haired woman draped in violet muslin stood at his elbow and stared mutely at Vivienne, though whether she was awe-stricken or upset, I couldn't say. She was well into her third decade, or perhaps her fourth, but her striking beauty hadn't faded in the least.

I sensed an undercurrent filled with past interactions I was not privy to.

And for that, I was glad.

"My *wife*, the baroness, is an admirer of yours, Miss Bloomfield-Smythe," the baron corrected her gently. "She was almost too shy to meet you, but I insisted we come over and at least congratulate you on your West End debut. We will surely attend in our usual box."

His wife? The baron must have been very wealthy or very powerful to have won who must have been an incredibly sought-after debutante in her day. And yet there had to be a minimum of two decades between the baron and baroness, if not three.

Vivienne took no time to process anything he'd said past the first couple of words. "Oh! Do pardon my faux pas," she insisted, laying her hand on the baron's lapel. "I should have known just by looking at her, that gown is positively prehistoric! Did it come from the same time period as yourself?"

A hush fell over the nearby assembly, a collective intake of breath at the bite of her words. The baron's face reddened beneath the white whiskers adorning his chin, but before he could muster a response, Vivienne had already moved to the next thought, leaving ripples of disquiet in her wake.

"Baron, I see you've plucked the short straw and are

obliged to conduct Herr Drumft around for the season." Vivienne motioned to the slightly rotund dignitary towering behind the baron, weighed down further by a sash cluttered with Prussian medals of some consequence and various other adornments.

"Your toy soldier seems ready to crumble," Vivienne mocked, pointing a slender finger toward Drumft, who stood as pinch-faced and unyielding as a marble statue. "Or perhaps that's merely the ground beneath him."

As Vivienne trilled a giggle at her own japes, a few joined her. Some behind their fans. Others nervously. And still more out of a sense of polite obligation.

I felt none of these things, and so didn't pretend to find her funny in the least.

I was beginning to wonder if we were watching a woman lose her sanity in front of the devil and everyone else gathered in Jorah's ballroom.

The baroness's nostrils flared ever so slightly, her cool composure a mask I knew belied a tempest brewing within. "Miss Bloomfield-Smythe, one's wit can cut deeper than any blade," she said, the portrait of dignified grace. "Pray, let us not turn this jovial gathering into a battlefield." The baroness kept her voice even, though the undercurrent of warning was clear as crystal.

"Battlefield?" Vivienne laughed, though the sound held no joy. "No, my dear baroness, the true fight lies beyond these gilded walls. Here"—she gestured to the

44

masquerade of decadence surrounding us—"we merely play at war."

Before the baroness could retort, Vivienne turned her cruel gaze upon Drumft, who watched the scene with hawklike intensity. His broad chest rose and fell beneath his impeccably tailored jacket and his scalp flushed an unnatural shade beneath painfully thin tufts of silver-blond hair.

"There'll be a battle soon enough in the ring," Darcy cut in, the tension in his shoulders belying the chirpy good nature in his tone. "Are you planning on attending the match as well, baron? Mr....Drumft, was it?"

"I will certainly be there." The man sniffed down his Germanic nose at Darcy, his clipped, accented words sounding more like a threat than an answer.

"I've a small fortune riding on it," the baron agreed, visibly relieved for a safer topic and a respite from Vivienne's verbal onslaught.

"Is that wise?" Vivienne asked, running a manicured finger around the rim of her third glass. "When the walls whisper, they say a *small* fortune is all you've left in the coffers."

At that, Darcy took her elbow in a none-too-gentle grip. "Now, Viv. Even *I* know it's gauche to tease about money in such company."

She whirled on him, eyes blazing. "You speak to me of gauche when we stand in the one structure that would make Sodom and Gomorrah look like a midnight mass in comparison? When a cretin like Herr Drumft is welcome to lurk in the shadows?" Her smile turned into a snarl as she addressed the portly Prussian. "Tell me, Oswald, do you wait like a dog beneath the table for your victims to throw you scraps, or have you finally managed to convince these people you're not a common beast?" Vivienne's voice dripped with venom, her insult echoing in alarming fractals over the swell of the music.

Drumft's jaw clenched, and his hands balled into fists at his sides. "There are some beasts one would do well not to provoke, Miss Bloomfield," he replied, his enunciation sharp as a knife's edge.

Vivienne's laugh was a cruel purr, and a twisted smile playing upon her rouged lips. "But where would be the fun in that?"

"Toying with certain people can be dangerous," the baroness warned, dark eyes intense and unblinking. "You've risen so fast to fame. Are you not afraid such behavior could lead to infamy? That another, more civilized woman would overtake you should scandal arise?"

Vivienne's laughter sang over the melodious strings as she breezed away with an air wave. "Overtake me? Now, my dear baroness, they'd have to catch me first," she said before chasing the footman with the champagne tray into the throng of bodies and out of sight.

Darcy cleared his throat before dipping his head to look down at me, then out to the scowling handful of people who'd been privy to Vivienne's behavior. "I-I suppose I should go after her." He chuckled. "She can get a bit...diabolical on anything with bubbles."

I hadn't realized Mr. Tyndall had found us until he trailed Darcy into the crowd like a long wraith.

They left behind a trail of disquiet, and I blinked after them until I felt the weight of many eyes upon me.

"Are you also an...associate of Mr. O'Dowd's, my dear?" The baroness skewered me with those dark, dark eyes, and I suddenly wanted to be anywhere in the world but in this ballroom.

"Just—the younger sister of an old friend from back home." I leaned into my Irish accent, the edges of which had been smoothed by my time in London. "Here for a night in a borrowed dress."

"How nice for you." As was my hope, I was readily dismissed with icy politeness as they formed a tightly knit group to whisper their displeasures to one another.

Left to my own devices, I decided to procure some champagne of my own. I'd a respectable wine collection at home, but nothing of the kind that Jorah could afford.

Beneath the crystal chandeliers dripping with opulence, I couldn't help but feel the shadow of dread creeping into the ballroom, its icy fingers brushing against my spine. The night was young, but a darkness within it had taken root, spreading its sinister tendrils through the revelry.

As if by design, the chandeliers dimmed as the night deepened. Gloves came off. Jackets and wraps were discarded, white ties pulled loose. The dancers pressed their bodies closer and gulped champagne by the crate.

My gaze found Jorah's once more in the crowd. He was, as usual, surrounded by sirens and sycophants, none of whom I wished to make an acquaintance with. He motioned to the balcony above the grand staircase with his head, and I took it to mean he planned to meet me there.

I was asked to dance twice on my way to the stairs, and twice I was obliged to accept.

My first partner wanted to talk about nothing but Darcy, and my second spoke very little English, while I understood no Spanish.

By the time I finally made my way to the landing, Jorah was nowhere to be found.

I checked the grandfather clock, and the night had rounded one thirty and was creeping toward two. It had descended into a muted hum of unease, the earlier exuberance curdling like sour milk. I opened my ear to the elite, their whispers knitting a shroud of foreboding that draped over the gilded ballroom. The clinking of crystal and swishing of silk did little to mask a growing sense of concern.

I touched a glittering matron on the arm as she passed me. "Pardon, but do you know what's going on?"

"I can hardly believe," she breathed. "Vivienne Bloomfield-Smythe, the night's brightest star, has vanished from our midst."

"Where could she be?" a dowager muttered behind a feathered fan, eyes darting like a caged bird. "It isn't like her to miss her own...spectacle."

The laughter had died, the music now a haunting lament as couples ceased their waltzing, their gazes turning toward the grand staircase where Vivienne had last been seen with a dismayed Darcy in her wake.

A cold prickle danced up my spine as I made my way through the sea of finery, each rustle of lace and pop of a champagne cork sounding a knell in the somber silence.

A hand closed like a vise around my arm. "Miss Mahoney." Jorah's voice held none of the languorous sensuality it often did when he spoke so close. The cold steel beneath his usual warmth lit a fire of warning in my belly. "We have a dire situation that demands your expertise."

I nodded in response, allowing Jorah to lead me through the curious crowd. My heart raced as we slipped into a dark and shadowy corridor, hidden from prying eyes. I trusted Jorah to protect me, but my instincts were screaming with caution.

I only had one expertise to speak of.

If it was required...then someone was dead.

Chapter Four

The chill of the alcove seeped into my bones as I stared down at who was once Vivienne Bloomfield-Smythe.

She lay stretched out like a macabre offering, her eyes glassy and fixed upon some eternal secret. A great sword had been thrust through her sternum with such force it pinned her, supine, to the floor. A lake of darkness pooled around her, warm and viscous, mingling with the crimson silk of her gown. A stark contrast to the pallor of her bloodless skin.

"Night Horse found her like this," Jorah informed me, his voice devoid of emotion, as if discussing the weather rather than a gruesome murder. "He's off looking for Darcy and Tunstall. They're nowhere to be found."

My gaze shifted from Vivienne's body to the platform where an antique knight's armor should have been complete. It stood sentinel outside the alcove, a hollow metal ghost missing its sword. At another time, I might have admired the craftsmanship of a bygone era, but now it only served as a grim visual respite from the tableau made of Vivienne's violent death.

I did my best not to think of the heavy sword piercing my middle. The heft and weight of it. The blade blunted by years of disuse.

"Where are Darcy and Tunstall? Do you think they're hurt as well?" I asked, my throat tight, as much from fear for my childhood friend as from the stench of iron and death.

"Missing," he replied succinctly. "Nary a trace of either man." His gaze cut to me, sharp and hard. "You should change back into your gray work attire," he ordered me. "You'll clean. I'll return to the party and control any damage a scandal could cause. Whatever happens tonight, her body must *not* be found on the premises." His words were cold, callous, and the reminder of what kind of man he truly was made me bleakly glad we weren't able to finish what we'd started in the Shiloh room.

"Send for my assistant Hao Long," I told him with a gusty sigh, preparing myself for the grim task ahead.

The thought of anyone knowing I was here when this had happened sent a shiver down my spine.

"Of course," he agreed, his tone betraying none of the urgency or dread that thrummed through me like a second pulse.

The silence of the alcove was barely stirred by the arrival of Night Horse, his voice a dark omen amidst the shadows. "Neither Darcy nor Tunstall are on this floor or in the ballroom," he announced, the words hanging in the air like a death knell. "I will search further. Do you want me to send—"

"Later," Jorah commanded in clipped tones, his gaze fixed on Vivienne's lifeless form. "We deal with the body first." He nodded toward Vivienne, and for an instant, there was a crack in his steely façade—a glimmer of sorrow?

Of regret?

"Jorah," I said, my voice barely above a whisper, "did you know her well?"

"I knew her...once," he replied, his eyes distant, evading the truth as deftly as a shadow flees the light.

A new voice turned my blood to ice. "The Hammer stands over another dead woman... When will they ever learn better than to seek his company?"

Detective Grayson Croft filled the alcove doorway, large and imposing, his rugged visage etched with disgust and something akin to wrath.

With dark hair that culminated in a widow's peak, square features, and fists the size of sledgehammers, he was more striking than traditionally handsome. The scent of winter rain clung to his coat, mingling with the familiar aroma of his signature fragrant tobacco.

His Yorkshire accent wrapped around me like the winter rain and my pulse quickened, not solely out of fear. His gaze lingered on me just long enough to stir a warmth in my belly before it flared into indignation.

"Fiona Mahoney," he intoned with a sneer. "You're here dancing with danger? Or just enjoying being a gem amongst the muck?"

I usually thought of a swift retort for Detective Croft, but my wits were muddled trying to discern if he'd just criticized or complimented me.

"Detective," Jorah said smoothly, stepping between us, his eyes glinting with a danger that yearned to do more than dance. "We've only just discovered poor Miss Bloomfield-Smythe's unfortunate demise. How is it you've arrived so prematurely when there has been barely enough time to send for the authorities?"

"If you meant to send for me at all," Croft correctly muttered. "Scotland Yard received an anonymous note saying someone had been attacked at the Velvet Glove."

"Curious," I murmured, unable to suppress the bite in my tone in the presence of Croft. "How very expedient of them."

"Indeed," Jorah concurred, eyeing Croft with unveiled suspicion. "The only conclusion to make is that the killer sent the note."

Croft snorted his disdain with a dark glance at Night Horse.

One the assassin returned, unblinking.

"Conclusions are reached through evidence," Croft said.

"You'll find none to implicate me or mine," Jorah

retorted.

The tension between the men crackled like electricity, and I couldn't quite understand the depth of their animosity. There was a history I didn't know. Things said and unsaid between them I couldn't discern.

As Croft stepped away to examine the scene, Jorah leaned in close, his breath warm against my ear. "I'll ask you this once, Fiona. Was it you who summoned Croft?"

"Of course not," I replied, feeling the weight of their enmity. It dawned on me then: "He's right, you know," I said to Croft, mindful for the first time that I was wearing a dead woman's gown. "She left the ballroom shortly before she was found. Only the murderer could have known, could have penned that damnable note, because for it to reach you and for you to respond with such alacrity..."

Croft turned from Vivienne to tower over me, verdant eyes blazing like the Green Man's punishing glare. "Want to tell me what you're doing in this infernal den of shite? With him?" The distaste rolled off his tongue like thunder as he jammed a finger in Jorah's direction, and I bristled at his audacity.

"What we all were doing," I answered, holding his gaze with more difficulty than I'd wished. "I was dancing."

Croft looked at me, his eyes holding a storm of emotions I dared not decipher. And as I stood there, caught between the devil and the deep blue sea, I realized that the night's events had only just begun to unfurl their twisted skein. His voice was like steel wrapped in velvet, and I could feel the weight of his gaze upon me as if it were a physical touch. "When last did you see Miss Bloomfield-Smythe alive?"

I swallowed hard and glanced at her body. Arched slightly, as if to receive a lover.

Lovely, even in death.

"She caused quite the scene," I began, my voice steady despite the tumult within. "There she was, all fire and fury, flinging accusations like they cost nothing at all." The memories unfurled like dark ribbons as the night's events tripped artlessly from my tongue; Vivienne had been a storm, leaving embarrassment and shock in her wake. Baron and Baroness Morton, Darcy, Tunstall, Claudia, Drumft—even Jorah—all targets of her inebriated wrath.

"She stormed off after her outburst, and Darcy went after her—Tunstall followed shortly after, presumably to help," I finished.

"And the Hammer?" Croft pressed, his eyes narrowing just so.

"As far as I knew, Jor—Mr. Roth—remained in the ballroom when she stormed off." There it was—an alibi for the man whose intentions I could never truly discern.

"Yet he led you to the body," Croft countered, a calculated edge to his tone.

"True, but..." My words faltered, and Jorah stepped in with the grace of a predator.

"Vivienne wasn't short on enemies tonight," he interjected smoothly, his gaze arrested by her cooling corpse. "She makes them as easily as she breathes."

Their eyes locked, and I sensed the coiled animosity ready to spring forth, a battle of wills that neither would concede.

The tension shattered as the door burst open, and Darcy, followed by Tunstall, stumbled into the room. Darcy's eyes skittered over each of us until he found Vivienne.

A guttural cry tore from his throat. A primal agony was etched across his features—a man beholding his world undone.

"Vivienne!" His voice cracked with despair, and he surged forward, only for Croft to intercept him with an iron grip. "Get away from her!"

"Stay back!" Croft barked.

As if fueled by pure instinct, Darcy swung at Croft, the sound of the impact like a gunshot in the tense room. Blood bloomed on Croft's lip, but he recovered with a roar and dove like a bull into Darcy's middle.

They fell to the ground, a tangle of limbs and fury, until Croft emerged on top, his hand snapping shut the irons on Darcy's thick wrists with a chilling finality.

"You're under arrest for assaulting an officer of the law," Croft spat, his face a mask of righteous anger. "And on suspicion of the murder of Vivienne Bloomfield-Smythe."

"Croft, no!" The plea ripped from my chest before I

could stop it. "You can't think Darcy did this! It's too soon to know any such thing."

But the detective's gaze was implacable, the judgment already cast in the grim set of his mouth. "You just told me they ran after her, then disappeared until her body was found."

"Yes, but I thought they might be victims!" I cried, putting my hand against Darcy's chest as if that could stop Croft from leading him away.

The big fighter's eyes flowed with moisture as he wept, openly, threatening to tear a hole in my heart.

Croft sidestepped my plea and shoved Darcy at an awaiting officer. "Lock him up," he said, his voice betraying no hint of the turmoil that must surely rage beneath. "And don't let the manager out of your sight."

"Stop! Let me see her! What happened to her? I did not do this! Vivienne!" As Darcy was dragged from the room, his eyes met mine—full of pain, betrayal, and a desperate plea for understanding. In that look, there was a story untold, a mystery wrapped in grief and fury. I knew then that the truth of this night was far from simple. But something deep in my soul whispered that truth lived inside of Darcy O'Dowd. "Fiona! You have to believe me!"

"Wait!" I cried out, desperation lending urgency to my voice. "You cannot arrest him without proper evidence."

"The note I received indicated that Mr. O'Dowd had committed the crime," Croft informed me, his tone clipped and cold as he swiped at his swelling lip with a pristine handkerchief, leaving a smear of crimson.

"Grayson." My voice was a hushed entreaty, threading through the thick tension in the room as I silently willed him to remember that we'd worked closely in the past. That I'd saved his sister from death, and that might buy me a little of his hard-won grace. "I know he hit you, but he is mad with grief. Darcy is not capable of this. I've known him almost my entire life, since he was a boy, and—"

"Capability is a fickle friend to innocence, Fiona," he interjected, his accent thickening with emotion, "and childhood connections often wither under the harsh truths of adulthood."

His words stung, a reminder of the gulf of years that lay between the boy I knew and the man accused. I stepped closer, the gown's emerald silk whispering against the stone floor, a stark contrast to the grim scene.

Why wouldn't he look at me for more than a glance?

"Nobody witnessed him do harm to her, Croft. Not one soul."

"Yet it is what lies unseen that often holds the key to justice." He handed me a crumpled note, the paper's edges smeared with ink. "This missive claims otherwise."

I unfolded it with trembling hands, the script dancing before my eyes—a chilling accusation pointing to Darcy. "But anyone could have penned this deceit."

"Could be deception," Croft conceded. "Could be a terrified witness. Nevertheless, I must follow where evidence leads. And it has led me here, to him."

"Then let it lead you further," I implored, my heart hammering a frantic rhythm. "Do not tether an innocent man to a crime he may not have committed."

"I will find the truth, Miss Mahoney, and mete out justice. In due time, I shall come to interrogate you as well. Stay close to home and expect my call."

The chill of the chamber seemed to seep into my very marrow as I watched Grayson Croft's broad, stalwart form, his back to me, the lines of his coat taut with restrained fury. His gaze lingered on where Darcy had been led away—a man now shackled and broken—before he turned his attention back to the bloody tableau before us.

"I'll be finished searching the scene for clues directly, Miss Mahoney. The coroner will let you know when you can begin."

I'd been summarily dismissed.

The scent of blood mingled with the faint traces of tobacco and rainwater as I turned on my heel and glided away from the grisly scene.

And with the weight of the night heavy upon me, I knew there would be no rest until the truth, however dark, was dragged into the merciless light of day.

UPON MY RETURN from changing back into my everyday gray frock, I found that the coroner's men had come to take the body. With their grim faces and methodical indifference, they wrapped the remains of Vivienne in a white shroud that seemed too pure for the scene it veiled.

Vivienne's young maid, Claudia, her figure bent as if to mirror the curvature of her grief, wept beside the alcove. Her small hands clutched at the empty air where her mistress had once been.

I approached carefully, Hao Long several silent steps behind me with the implements to ply our gruesome trade. "Are you—" I cleared awkwardness out of my throat. "Is there someone that can be contacted to collect you?" I asked as kindly as I could.

"Miss Bloomfield-Smythe was everything," Claudia murmured through tears that painted glistening trails down her cheeks. "She was all I had."

"Don't fret—Claudia, was it?" Jorah's voice was softer than I'd ever heard it, though it did little to mask the steel within. He placed a hand upon her quivering shoulder, an anchor in the tide of her sorrow. "You'll stay under my roof tonight, Claudia. We'll find a place for you and sort it all out in the light of day."

I should have been as comforted as Claudia seemed to be, but I knew Jorah's place for women was sometimes as a prostitute in one of his houses.

He turned to me then, his brow furrowed in consternation. "Unlike you, I've been summoned *immediately* to

Scotland Yard. Though I'm no stranger to their inquiries, I'll not walk into that den without my solicitor."

"Will you be all right?" I asked, more out of courtesy than concern.

"Always," he replied, his lips curling into a half-smile that never reached his eyes. "But tell me, Fiona, do you believe Darcy capable of such savagery?"

I hesitated, feeling the weight of his gaze like a physical thing. "I want to believe in his innocence," I confessed. "But I—"

"Say no more." His expression darkened. "I stand to lose much if he's guilty—this exhibition match was to be a culmination of no small efforts. Not just for Darcy, but for me as well. For men even more brutal than I."

A silence fell between us, filled only by the distant murmur of the party, unaware or uncaring of the death that lingered in our midst. Then, with a nod that seemed final, Jorah strode away, leaving me to confront the remnants of the night's horror in order to empty the Velvet Glove of revelers.

"Miss Fiona," came the low drawl of Hao Long, his silk-clad form materializing from the gloom. His aged face bore the marks of one who had seen much yet spoke little of it.

"Mr. Long," I greeted him, offering a weak smile as I approached the cart laden with bottles and cloths, each a silent testament to the nature of our work. "We have a task before us."

Hao nodded, his movements precise as he handed me gloves. Together, we began the somber ritual of erasing death's handiwork. As I scrubbed at the crimson pool, I wondered if it was possible to cleanse the stain from my soul as easily as from the floor.

"Thank you," I whispered to Hao, who merely inclined his head and continued his meticulous work. In this world of secrets and lies, of violence woven into the fabric of our lives, there were few people I trusted. Hao Long, with his quiet strength and unspoken understanding, was one of them.

And as the scent of hypochlorite rose to mingle with the lingering traces of perfume and metal, I felt the familiar pull of the darkness that lurked within the heart of the city—and within me. My thoughts churned like the stormy London skies overhead, heavy with doubt and suspicion. Each swipe of my cloth seemed to peel away another layer of deception, revealing a deeper, darker truth beneath.

"Miss Mahoney," Hao called softly, drawing my attention to an object he'd found wedged beneath the armor's decorative platform. It was a delicate lace handkerchief, stained crimson with Vivienne's blood. But what truly caught my eye was the embroidered initials in one corner—*C.F.*

"Clarissa Fairchild, the Baroness Morton," I whispered, my heart quickening at the implication. The baroness had motive, her social standing threatened by Vivienne, yet this single clue did little to exonerate

Darcy. In fact, it only served to thicken the web of intrigue that surrounded us all.

"Keep this hidden for now, Hao Long," I instructed him, my voice barely audible above the unsettling silence that had fallen over the Velvet Glove. He nodded solemnly, tucking the handkerchief into an envelope that I slid into my pocket.

My mind raced as we finished cleaning the alcove, the ghosts of those who may have wanted Vivienne dead swirling around me. The baron, whose reputation was tarnished by her antics; the baroness, whose very position in society was jeopardized by Vivienne's presence; Drumft, embittered and resentful of her; Tunstall, harboring ill will toward her closeness to Darcy. And then there was Darcy himself, the childhood friend whose innocence I desperately yearned to prove.

But who hated her enough to kill her?

I set to work, every scrub a strike against the chaos that threatened to engulf us all.

I was glad Jorah had left, his charm and poise a mask that would see him safely home with no legal ramifications, I was sure.

I knew too well the monster that lurked beneath that suave exterior—the same monster that had almost lured me into its web.

"Almost" being the operative word.

As the last of the blood washed away, I felt a twinge of satisfaction. Tonight, I had escaped the clutches of one monster, only to clean up after another.

Chapter Five

The chill of the Scotland Yard holding cells crept beneath my shawl, a spectral whisper against my skin as I navigated the dim corridors. A sense of foreboding hung like cobwebs in the damp air, adding weight to each step I took toward Darcy's cell.

I paused at the threshold, finding Tunstall's imposing form hovering over Darcy like a raven circling carrion. His voice was a murmur, conspiratorial and urgent, and it scraped against my nerves like a blade. I was not meant to overhear their dialogue; that much was certain.

Darcy rose from the cot, his stature diminished by the confines but not his spirit. His eyes brightened when they met mine, a spark of life amidst the gloom. "Fiona," he said, and even through the bars, his presence enveloped me, comforting and familiar. "I didn't think to see you here, so close to the devil's frigid arse."

"Miss Mahoney." Tunstall's greeting was as sharp and unwelcome as a splinter. His eyes, the color of tarnished silver, flicked toward me, betraying his discontent before his lips curled into a semblance of courtesy.

"Mr. Tunstall," I replied, my voice steadier than I felt. The cramped cell seemed to shrink further at my intrusion, the walls resonating with the tension that hummed between the two men.

"Jesus, Mary, and Joseph, Fiona, I can't believe this is real." Darcy began to pace like a ship in a storm, erratic and directionless. "Flynn would have known what to do," he said, his voice catching as he invoked my brother's name, wrapping his fingers around the bars as his eyes pleaded with mine. "We had grand times, the lot of us, didn't we? Finn, Flynn, Aidan, and me. You and Mary. Running wild on the moors, chasing secrets..."

"Those were different days," I whispered, the memories bittersweet on my tongue.

"Flynn... God rest him," Darcy said, bowing his head with a reverence that spoke of shared grief. "He and I, we were thick as thieves. And when they... When he was taken from us, strung up like an animal for England's cruel spectacle—it was a wrong that can never be set right."

A sorrowful silence stretched between us, the echo of our past losses binding us tighter than any conspiracy could. I fought back the surge of emotions threatening to overwhelm me, the raw ache for my brothers and the life we could never reclaim.

"Fi," Darcy began, his voice a warming balm against the coldness of the room. He was a towering figure even within the confines of his cage, his broad shoulders casting shadows in the flickering gaslight. "You came to see me in the wee hours. Does that mean you believe me innocent?"

"I find it impossible to believe that you'd have hurt Vivienne," I answered, as close to the truth as I could get.

Darcy's eyes—a deep, Baltic blue—lit up with a mingling of hope and gratitude. His large, calloused hands reached through the bars for my own. "Georgie here was just saying how you've unraveled mysteries before. That you've been in the papers. Is that true?"

"Mr. Tunstall exaggerates my skills," I remarked dryly. I didn't miss the way Tunstall's jaw tightened at the mention of his name or the dark glint in his eye when he looked at Darcy.

Darcy's face was just as I remembered it. Open. Simple. Earnest. "Do you... I can't even in good conscience ask...but I've precious few allies in this fetid city. Can you help me clear me name? I'll pay you, whatever your fee."

"I don't know," I answered honestly. "I clean up after murder scenes and...sometimes I find something that pulls me into the investigation." I pressed the handkerchief through the cold iron. It unfurled like a white flag of truce between us. "This might help keep your chin up, though. I found it snagged on the knight's suit of armor."

The handkerchief fluttered in my hand like a specter, its lace edges gently frayed from wear and worry. The baroness's monogram, a delicate *C.F.* embroidered in silver thread, shimmered in the dim light of Darcy's cell.

"Fi," he whispered, his voice hoarse with emotion, "this could be it—the very thing to clear me."

I felt the pulse of his hope, the thrumming life beneath his skin. It was infectious, this belief that one piece of cloth might unravel the web of lies entangling him. My own heart quickened at the prospect, the dormant fire within me kindled anew by the right-eousness of our cause.

"Then we must ensure it finds its way into the right hands," I said resolutely, my resolve hardening like the cobblestones beneath the city's grimy veneer.

"Thank you, Fiona." Darcy's gaze held mine, an ocean of gratitude and history swirling in his eyes. "For believing in me, for everything..."

"Stop your thanks until we've won your freedom," I chided, though my chest swelled with the weight of our shared past. Flynn's laughter echoed in the hollows of my memory, Darcy by his side, always the champions of my youthful escapades. Flynn's absence was a gaping wound, but in Darcy's presence, the edges seemed less ragged.

"Remember the moors, Fi?" Darcy's question pulled me back into the now, the sharp tang of peat and heather filling my senses. "We were invincible there."

"Invincible," I echoed, the word bitter on my tongue. We had been children, untouched by death. But then the world had shown us its true face, painted in the blood of those we loved.

A pall of silence draped around us as the clank of iron heralded an arrival. Steps echoed through the dank corridor, deliberate and heavy, like the gavel of fate itself.

"O'Dowd," Croft's baritone rumbled, surprise coloring his tone as his gaze landed not on some faceless visitor, but on me. "I didn't expect to find Miss Mahoney in your company."

"Nor did I," I murmured, a chill skittering down my spine. The notion that he might have overheard our exchange—overheard talk of my family—coiled in my stomach like a serpent. I held his gaze, challenging, defiant. "Have you been listening at keyholes again, detective?"

"Merely cautious," he replied, the corners of his mouth twitching with something akin to amusement— or was it disdain? "I was told O'Dowd had a comely female visitor. I thought it warranted investigation. Little did I know you'd be here sharing secrets."

"Secrets," I scoffed softly, letting the word linger between us, thick with implication. My family's end was no secret, yet it was a tale I preferred to keep cloistered within my own heart, away from English lips that could twist it into justification for their savagery.

"You've made your discovery," I said, steeling myself against the memories that threatened to break free. "Now, if you'll excuse us—"

"Actually, I won't," Croft cut in, stepping closer. His shadow loomed over us, a specter of authority. "I've been quite clear, Fiona. You are not to involve yourself in this investigation."

"Clear as the Thames," I quipped, flapping the handkerchief beneath his nose—the delicate fabric now a player in our grim theater. "I found this at the murder scene beneath the knight's feet. Look at what is embroidered here—C.F.—could stand for Clarissa Fairchild, don't you think? Surely that's a clue pointing in a direction other than Darcy's."

Tunstall shifted beside me, his muscles tensing, his eyes darting to the handkerchief with a flicker of...what? Recognition? Fear? It unsettled me, the way he seemed to shrink before the monogrammed cloth as if it were a harbinger of doom rather than a mere piece of linen.

"Put that away," he said, a touch too vehement before he caught himself. "Women drop their handkerchiefs about everywhere. That's hardly a clue."

"Do they?" My voice was calm, belying the turmoil within. The initials whispered of connections unseen, a web of intrigue that ensnared us all. "One would think you'd be happy for anything that might point the finger away from your client, Mr. Tunstall."

"Enough," Croft intervened. "This is police evidence, not a parlor game, and you, Miss Mahoney, are coming with me."

His grip was firm yet not unkind as he grasped my elbow and steered me from the gloom of Darcy's cell through the labyrinth of Scotland Yard. The staircases seemed endless, spiraling upward like the coiled entrails of the building itself, each step echoing with our ascent. I could feel the eyes of constables and inspectors upon us, their whispers trailing along the stone walls, as elusive as the hint of mist that clung to my woolen coat.

"Up here," Croft said tersely as we reached his domain, a spartan room where justice was administered with an iron pen. His desk stood like an altar amid the stifling silence, papers strewn across its surface like offerings to some bureaucratic deity.

The scent of ink and aged paper pervaded the floor, a stark contrast to the musty decay of the cells below. The lamplight flickered as a draft whispered through the poorly sealed windows, casting elongated shadows across his furrowed brow. He regarded me with an intensity that would have made a weaker woman quail.

"Miss Mahoney," Croft began, his voice low, "you said you believe this handkerchief belongs to the baroness?"

"Perhaps," I replied, unfurling the delicate fabric between my fingers. "Or perhaps it's a clever misdirection." My eyes darted to his, igniting with the thrill of the chase. "Imagine the scandal if it were not. She's not the only person in attendance I suspect of the murder."

Croft leaned back in his chair, the leather creaking beneath him. "Go on," he prompted, skepticism etched into the hard lines of his face.

"Consider Drumft," I said, pacing before his desk. The memories of the night swirled within my mind, each player a suspect in their own right. "A foreign dignitary of influence and prestige. She said some awful things about him in front of everyone, and we know how dangerous a humiliated man can be."

"As a motive, it's thin," Croft conceded, tapping his pen against a stack of papers. "Herr Drumft is steeped in and surrounded by scandals of the highest order, and none of it seems to muddy the hem of his cloak. Did you see him leave the ballroom?"

I hadn't.

"There's Baron and Baroness Morton." I stopped pacing, turning to face him fully. "Their marriage—a bastion of society, yet built on foundations of convenience. Vivienne, with her beauty and charm, would have been a threat to any woman, let alone one as cold and calculating as Lady Clarissa Fairchild. Perhaps she and the baron have history. It's at least worth looking into."

"True," he murmured, scribbling notes. "I already planned to check if Miss Bloomfield-Smythe was... socially connected to the baron. But, Fiona, people like these... They rarely commit their own violence. They're more likely to hire it done." He stood, relieving himself of his jacket and draping it over the back of his chair.

For some reason I found myself arrested by the color of his arm through the starch white of his shirt. A silhouette of flesh and muscle able to grapple a prize-fighter to the ground.

And win.

"We have to consider that C and F are not uncommon initials, and this flower..." Croft picked up the handkerchief and ran a rough thumb over the embossed bloom of pale stitches. "I feel like I've seen it somewhere before."

"Let's not forget Claudia, her maid," I blurted, as a thought occurred to me. "Vivienne treated her abominably, and the girl licked at her boots like a kicked puppy. Adoration can fester, detective. It can turn love into something dark and twisted."

"An obsession turned violent," Croft mused, nodding grimly. "Wouldn't have been easy for the slip of a girl to stage a scene like that. Doubt she could lift that sword, let alone wield it."

True.

I bit my lip while I thought.

"The Hammer is high on the suspect list," he speculated, sliding a sly glance in my direction. "He operates in secrets and silence. And Vivienne betrayed him, stole from him once upon a time. If anyone has a long enough memory to serve revenge this cold, it's Jorah David Roth."

"Yet Jorah wouldn't leave loose ends," I pointed out. "He'd ensure no trail led back to him."

"You're saying you believe him capable of murder." Croft crossed his hands over his wide chest, menace rolling from his entire body. "And still you revel in his midnight masquerades."

I *knew* Jorah to be a killer, though I understood he never considered his actions murder.

I very much doubted Croft appreciated the nuance and wisely held my tongue.

"What about George Tunstall?" I said, my gaze hardening. "You see the way he slithers around Darcy, always lurking in the shadows. There's more than just dislike for Vivienne there. Jealousy, perhaps? Or something more sinister?"

"Greed is a powerful motive," Croft agreed, leaning forward, intrigued despite himself. "As manager he gets a percentage, and he only makes money if O'Dowd does. What would Tunstall have to gain by imprisoning his own prizefighter?

"You're the detective," I said, locking eyes with him. "Go detect!"

"Only if you go home and wait for my interrogation."

"I'm here now." I opened my arms. "Interrogate me."

"I'll take your entire statement in my own time, but I am aware that your...*opinions* are compromised by depth of feeling for your pugilist."

"He's not *my* anything," I spat. "He is—was—my

brother Flynn's best mate and one of the only tethers I've left to my home."

Silence settled between us as the gravity of the situation took hold. I wandered to the window, peering into the murky London street below. The gas lamps threw their feeble light against the encroaching fog, battling back the darkness that sought to claim the city's soul.

"Be careful, Fiona," Croft said, a rare note of concern lacing his words. "This is a dangerous game you're playing."

"Isn't it always?" I retorted without looking back, my thoughts already spiraling toward the night ahead. In the gloom of my resolve, I felt the pull of the abyss, the sweet seduction of enigma beckoning me closer.

"You're going to keep Darcy imprisoned, then?" I asked crisply, turning from the dark.

"For now," was his cryptic reply.

"Then you can't stop me from doing whatever it takes to procure his release," I said over my shoulder as I snatched the handkerchief from him and flounced away.

I'd put half of Scotland Yard's night shift in between the two of us before he sprang from his desk and made it out of his office to bellow after me.

I ignored him, of course.

The heavy door of Scotland Yard clanged shut behind me, a reverberating echo of solitude as I descended the stone steps. The air was thick with fog, a shroud that veiled the city in mystery and malice. My boots clicked against the cobblestones in steady rhythm, an undercurrent to the tumultuous thoughts storming within my mind.

A handkerchief, a flower—an emblem of nobility and secrecy entwined. The tiniest of threads could unravel the most intricate of tapestries.

And I had very little time to do so before Croft caught me up and demanded the handkerchief back for evidence.

I halted beneath the archway of an alley, the scent of rain on stone filling my senses, mingling with the faint odor of decay that seemed ever-present in this city of contrasts. My mind was a whorl of thoughts, each vying for dominance, yet all centered around one immutable fact:

I seem to be forever fated to chase murderers through the dark streets of London.

Chapter Six

❦

The metallic tang of death hung thick in the air of the West End morgue, mingling with the stench of formaldehyde and decay.

It was a place of deathly science: walls lined with ceramic tiles, gleaming under the flickering gaslights, stark and white like the bleached bones of some leviathan beast. In the center lay the slab, a somber altar on which rested the mortal remains of Vivienne Bloomfield-Smythe, her flesh pale and exposed, dissected by the precise hands of Dr. Phillips. My heart clenched at the sight of her pale flesh marred by the Y-shaped incision that opened her torso.

"Ah, Miss Mahoney," came the voice of the doctor, his tone carrying the weight of knowledge and the sterility of his profession. "You've appeared as if I conjured you by thinking." Dr. Phillips stood hunched over the body, his wisps of white hair escaping the loose confines of his spectacles, a silhouette every bit the mad scientist from penny dreadfuls, save for the compassion I knew beat within his steady heart. "Tell me, my dear, have you come to peddle wares?"

The question rang ridiculous from a coroner plying his trade, but Dr. Phillips and I had a business relationship first and foremost. In the Venn diagram of our work, the overlap was sometimes unclaimed dead bodies. Medical colleges, hospitals, scientific researchers, and some private ventures paid unthinkable sums for a well-preserved corpse.

Dr. Phillips participated in the trade for the sake of science.

I participated for the sake of necessity.

"Actually, doctor, I've come to ask after Miss Bloomfield-Smythe." I traced the jagged line of stitches along Vivienne's abdomen with my gaze, unable to look away.

What secrets had her death revealed?

He directed a frown at me. "I did not assume you were acquaintances, Miss Mahoney, as I gather this... woman was a creature of the *demimonde* and prone to nefarious behavior."

"I admit I'm more acquainted with death than I was with Vivienne," I mused aloud, my thoughts drifting like mist. "But I was one of the last people to see her alive, and...she was kind to me."

If not to everyone else.

"Quite," he murmured, a small grunt accompanying

his agreement as he peered closer at something within Vivienne's chest cavity.

I approached the slab, my gaze drawn inexorably to the still figure. Her nakedness did not perturb me; it was the final truth laid bare, every secret etched upon her skin now a silent testament to her last moments. There was an artistry to the incisions, the neat flaps of skin pulled back to reveal the mysteries beneath. Most people would turn away, nauseated or horrified, but I found a strange solace in the clear-cut lines of reality.

"Any revelations yet?" I inquired, curious despite myself.

"Patience, Fiona," Dr. Phillips chided without malice. "One mustn't rush science. But there are peculiarities. Look here." He gestured with a bloodied finger, beckoning me closer.

Leaning in, I observed where his finger pointed—a bruise beneath the skin, hidden from a cursory glance. "What caused that?" My voice was a whisper, reverence for the departed mingling with the thrill of the hunt.

"Pressure," he stated. "A grip of some kind, perhaps. We'll know more soon."

"Vivienne had many secrets," I said, half to myself. "Would that she could tell us which one killed her."

"Secrets don't die, Miss Mahoney," Dr. Phillips replied, straightening to look at me with those piercing, analytical eyes. "They merely wait to be unearthed."

"Have you unearthed any of hers?"

With a heavy sigh, Phillips turned her neck. "The

cause of death was a blow to the back of the head. Not the sword, as was suspected."

"Someone hit her first?" My mind spun with implications. A crime of passion, then. Probably not premeditated.

"Yes. The sword was inserted postmortem, likely to mislead investigators Or...make a vulgar point of some significance." Phillips frowned, eying me over the rim of his spectacles. "Your presence at the Velvet Glove the night of Vivienne's demise is disconcerting." His tone was stern, though not unkind. "Rubbing shoulders with the likes of Jorah, the Hammer? There is a man who made a friend of death."

"Desperate times call for unsavory alliances," I confessed, avoiding his gaze. My mind flitted back to the sultry air of the Velvet Glove, the way the Hammer's eyes promised secrets and sin. The possessiveness of his lips underscored by skill and desire.

Needless to say, I indulged in no such detail with the good doctor.

An intrusive curiosity made me wonder if he'd an understanding of sexual desire past mere scientific curiosity and the biological imperative of the deed.

The door groaned like a beast, and in stepped Detective Croft, the scent of tobacco and bergamot trailing behind him like a smoky veil. The dim lighting in the morgue glinted off the gold badge on his chest and cast shadows on the angular lines of his face. His gaze flicked between myself and the gory tableau on the table before he allowed a frown to etch lines of disapproval in his brutal features.

"Miss Mahoney. I might have known you'd beat me here." Though his words held a hint of reproach, I detected a grudging respect in his tone. Croft didn't approve of my penchant for haunting crime scenes, but he couldn't deny my occasional usefulness.

"Detective." I inclined my head, ignoring how Croft's presence commanded the room, his confident strides silent on the linoleum floor. As he passed by, I could feel the subtle shift in the air, his tall frame creating a slight breeze that brushed against my skin. "Dr. Phillips has made some interesting discoveries."

Croft's gaze sharpened as he turned to the coroner. "Is that so, doctor?"

Phillips adjusted his spectacles, launching into a recitation of his findings. "The cause of death was not the sword wound, but rather a blow to the back of the head. There are indications the body was moved postmortem, as evidenced by—"

"The sword pinning her to the parquet." Croft's brow furrowed.

"Quite." Phillips slid a sidelong glance at Croft, and I could hear the cogs and wheels grinding as he considered the man. "Are there women in your suspect pool, detective inspector?" he queried.

Croft's eyes flicked to me before he answered in a thickening Yorkshire brogue, "Aye. Though not many. Why do you ask?"

Phillips pointed to the wound beneath Vivienne's previously coiffed hair. "Given the nature of the fracture, I would estimate the killer to be closer to our Miss Mahoney's height than to yours. I hope not to cause offense, dear, but there are not many men who proudly stand at your altitude."

"No offense taken," I said, squaring my shoulders and straightening my spine without strictly meaning to.

"The Dublin Destroyer is not more than a cricket's sneeze taller than Miss Mahoney," Croft said, demonstrating the man's height with the flat of his hand held at his chin.

"That proves nothing," I spat, turning to do my best job at looming *up* at him. "Miss Bloomfield-Smythe was a woman of many male acquaintances. Any number of them could be—vertically challenged."

"Her men I'm aware of are all well over six feet," Croft replied. "Drumft, the baron, Tunstall, and a handful of previous lovers and associates—of whom you are *not* aware because this is not your investigation, Miss Mahoney."

Dr. Phillips hummed beneath his breath as he worked, nimble fingers sorting through Vivienne's vitals with clinical detachment. "I'm not much involved in society scandals, but the only time I was made aware of Miss Bloomfield-Smythe's existence was when the papers placed her often in the company of His Royal Highness, Prince Albert Victor."

Croft and I both regarded the man with slack-jawed

astonishment. Queen Victoria's favored grandson? The heir *to the heir* to the throne?

Phillips went on without seeming to realize our shock—indeed, he might have been speaking to himself for all the notice he paid to us. "Of course, HRH is six foot and some more, but I suppose he could have hired it done. Though I don't see why. Rumors abound about our dear prince's proclivities, don't they?" He cleared a bit of scandal from his throat. "'Tis said he prefers the intimate company of men, and was quite the fixture of certain disreputable clubs rumored to cater to those with such predilections."

I stilled, stunned by this revelation. The royal family's secrets were closely guarded, and such gossip could be considered dangerous. "You should be careful to whom you reveal these rumors," I cautioned, checking Croft for any bouts of nationalism that might see Dr. Phillips arrested for treason.

"I don't spread rumors, Miss Mahoney—I analyze facts." The coroner glanced up and pushed his spectacles higher on his nose. "And the facts seem to indicate our prince moved in the same circles as the late Miss Bloomfield-Smythe. Circles both glittering and shadowed. Those shadows are likely enshrouding your murderer."

The implications were staggering. I shook my head in disbelief. "You can't seriously think the Prince of Wales's son is a suspect."

"In my experience, no one is above sin or suspicion."

Croft's tone brooked no argument. "We must follow the evidence, wherever it leads, even if it places a member of the royal family under the magnifying glass."

"The Crown will never stand for it," I warned.

A wolfish smile curled Croft's lips. "Then they shouldn't have left this case in my hands, should they?"

I stared at the mottled contusion marring Vivienne's pale flesh. A blow from something heavy and blunt, with enough force to crush bone.

"The killer is most likely right-handed. A single, efficient strike." Dr. Phillips fell back to the simple facts, though his gaze was troubled behind his spectacles. "An act of rage, not a crime of passion. The culprit likely knew and despised the victim."

Unease slithered down my spine as I met Croft's eyes. We were not dealing with merely a jealous lover or common footpad.

"We are hunting a killer driven by hatred and wrath," I said. "Darcy is neither of those things. I don't even recall his having a temper as a lad."

"Yet he punches people for a living," Croft pointed out, touching his still-swollen lip.

"Out of skill, not temper," I retorted.

"I don't disagree with you," Croft conceded. "I've no personal wish to see Darcy behind bars, Miss Mahoney. The man's prowess in the ring is unmatched. Still, I am bound by duty."

"Isn't your duty dictated by truth? There is enough evidence to suggest there are others from Vivienne's

A VOCATION OF VIOLENCE

past who warrant scrutiny. People with motives every bit as strong as Darcy's."

My mind raced, sorting through the tangled web of secrets and scandal surrounding Vivienne's life. There were too many suspects with motive enough to wish her harm.

"Darcy is a statistically probable place to begin," Croft insisted. "He has the possible motive, means, and the opportunity, and he refuses to give me an alibi. But I'll grant you that half of London society had reason to loathe Vivienne Bloomfield-Smythe."

I didn't know Darcy hadn't an alibi, even a flimsy one, for where he was those missing minutes between when he chased Vivienne from the ballroom to when he was seen again after her discovery.

I met Croft's gaze steadily. "Where would you suggest to start looking, detective?"

Croft studied me for a long moment, eyes hooded. I couldn't decipher his expression, but something in his regard made me shift uncomfortably.

At last, he said, "*I* shall start with those who stood to gain most from Vivienne's death. Her rival lovers, or those whose secrets she held as weapons. The baroness comes to mind, given her fixation on elevating her own status by tearing others down. And this mysterious royal connection you mentioned..."

He trailed off, scowling.

"There is always her maid, Claudia," Croft continued. "She's a slightly built girl, and her obsession with

Vivienne seems to have curdled into a resentful sort of love. She is unbalanced, and may have killed in a fit of madness and jealousy. We should look into her whereabouts at the time of the murder."

"And Jorah?" I said softly. My pulse quickened at the mere thought of that dangerous man. The memory of his touch, his kiss, still haunted my dreams—and now my waking hours as well.

Croft's gaze sharpened. "You seem unusually eager to accuse your...friend." His tone held a biting edge. "Has he given you cause to distrust him in this matter?"

I flushed under the implied censure, lowering my eyes. How could I explain my tangled feelings for Jorah, the seductive thrill of danger he represented and the forbidden passion we shared?

Croft would never understand.

"You seemed happy enough to accuse him the night of. I only wish to consider every possibility," I said stiffly. "Jorah knew Vivienne, and I'm led to believe their affair ended poorly."

"As you say." Croft's reply was noncommittal. "We shall look into every possibility, no matter how... *unpalatable.*"

His pointed emphasis made the heat in my cheeks blaze higher. But I refused to be ashamed for following the truth, no matter where it led.

Even if it led me to ruin.

"You'll be glad to know that we're releasing O'Dowd until better evidence surfaces, though he's not to leave London under any circumstances," he told me.

"Good." A relieved sigh slipped from my chest, mingling with the chill air of the morgue. The notion that Darcy could languish behind bars for a crime I knew his heart too pure to commit was as unbearable as the frigid steel beneath my fingertips.

"You know, some year or so past there was quite the scandal," Dr. Phillips muttered, almost to himself, with an uncharacteristic glint in his eye. "Prince Albert Victor was reputed to be a card-carrying member of the Order of the Green Carnation."

"Order of the what now?" Detective Croft asked, his voice a low rumble.

"An underground society of some infamy," Phillips recalled. "For men who favor the—er—intimate companionship of other men. One must ponder the implications if Miss Bloomfield-Smythe was privy to such secrets or in possession of the proof."

"If she used this information for blackmail, it would give the Crown motive to kill her," Croft replied. "The scandal of that magnitude, alone, might be enough to force his removal from the line of succession."

"The most powerful motive yet," I whispered.

"And eminently unprovable," Croft lamented. "Investigating the royal connection will be...problematic." His face hardened, etched with the lines of a man bracing for an inevitable storm.

"Problematic?" I echoed, raising an eyebrow. His

reluctance piqued my interest; there was more at stake than mere propriety.

"Career suicide," he admitted, flicking his gaze toward Dr. Phillips, who hummed in agreement. "Digging too deep into royal affairs... Well, one risks being buried by them."

"Yet if justice demands it, you'll proceed?" My respect for the detective grew as I watched him wrestle with the decision. It was one thing to chase shadows in back alleys, quite another to drag them from palatial halls.

"Justice," Croft affirmed, his voice low and resolute as he donned his overcoat and bade us good day with a grim set to his hard mouth.

Once he had departed, leaving a silence punctuated only by the distant echo of his footsteps, Dr. Phillips turned to me, his expression shifting from somber to pragmatic.

"Is the Ripper a specter that hangs over Miss Bloomfield-Smythe, Fiona?" he asked with uncharacteristic intensity. "You're not likely to attach to such a messy case unless the hunt is afoot."

I shook my head. "For once, doctor, this is purely personal. Darcy O'Dowd was a dear friend as a child, and I've not many connections left to my home. He is one of the happy few, and I can't rest until I've done my best by him."

He looked as if he were about to pat my hand before remembering what still stained his fingers a deep red.

"I've no right to ask you to look after yourself, but I will all the same," he said without looking up. "The shadows around this woman are deeper than your usual fare, as are the pockets of the players." His stitching hand paused. "Money makes bodies disappear, Fiona. As you well know."

"I'll be careful," I promised, warming at the concern he wasn't comfortable expressing.

As I left the morgue, the oppressive air of death clung to me like a second skin. I pondered the suspects —Jorah with his criminal empire, Claudia with her obsessive adoration, the baroness with her cold ambition—and wondered whether justice could truly prevail when power and privilege clouded the truth.

At least I knew someone who could answer so many of the questions burning a hole in my chest.

And he happened to live right next door to me.

Chapter Seven

The air, heavy with the promise of rain, clung to my skin as I approached the grand townhouse on Tite Street. It stood proudly next to mine. The eccentric décor, a cornucopia of flora and fauna motifs, spoke volumes of the man who resided within its walls.

I rapped my knuckles on the ornate door, feeling the familiar trepidation that often accompanied my visits. The man inside was brilliant, but his mind was a labyrinth I could never quite navigate with certainty.

The door swung open, revealing fellow Irishman Oscar Wilde himself, clad in a velveteen smoking jacket that matched the merry twinkle in his eyes.

"Ah, dear Fiona," he said, greeting me with a flourish. "I find that the only way to get rid of a temptation is to yield to it. And so, here you stand at my doorstep. Please, do come in."

"Thank you, Oscar," I replied, kissing his offered cheek and stepping into the lavishly furnished parlor, a veritable treasure trove of curiosities and oddities. I marveled at the sheer audacity of his taste, the paradoxical marriage of opulence and whimsy.

"Would you care for some coffee?" he asked, motioning to a porcelain pot perched atop a silver tray. "I've only tea made, but I remember your penchant for the devil's brew."

"Tea would be just fine," I said, watching as he poured the steaming liquid into an intricate cup. He handed it to me with a knowing smile, as if privy to some secret I had yet to decipher.

"Please, have a seat." He gestured toward an elegant settee draped in sumptuous fabrics. I sank into the plush cushions, feeling the weight of my worries ease ever so slightly.

"Oscar, I need your advice," I began before sipping the tea, feeling its warmth spread through me. "There are certain...matters that have arisen which require a perspective beyond my own."

"Ah," he said, leaning back in his armchair and studying me with an intensity that sent shivers down my spine. "It is said that 'to define is to limit,' but I shall endeavor to assist you nonetheless."

"Your insight has always been invaluable, Oscar," I replied gratefully, my thoughts turning to the tangled web of secrets and betrayals that had led me here.

I settled into the plush armchair, feeling the weight

of my burdens lighten ever so slightly in the sanctuary of Oscar's parlor. The array of colors and curiosities surrounding us served as a peculiar contrast to the dark mysteries that plagued me. Oscar was well aware of my profession, though he often considered death a lark rather than a loss.

"Oscar," I began, my voice hushed and urgent, "I must delve deeper into the lives of a few socialites that move in circles closer to yours than mine. Vivienne Bloomfield-Smythe and Clarissa Fairchild, the Baroness Morton."

His gray eyes glinted with dark pleasure. "Tell me you weren't at the Velvet Glove when poor Viv was butchered!"

"You knew Miss Bloomfield-Smythe, then?" I asked, my own heartbeat speeding with a gleeful relief.

"Well, we buy our cocaine from the same people," he said, flapping his hand over his face as if to dispel a distasteful aroma. "If I'm honest, she sparkled too bright to share a table with me, darling, as we'd blind everyone in the room."

I gave a wry laugh, despite myself, enjoying Oscar entirely, as one could not help but to do.

I knew that his information would come with a price, one I paid readily, divulging all I saw and heard that fateful night at the Velvet Glove.

Listening raptly, Oscar collapsed against the chaise when I finished my account, lighting a cigarette like a replete lover.

"Ah, our dear Vivienne and the baroness," he mused, reclining like a languid feline. "The whispers that surround them are as numerous as the stars, but only few hold a semblance of truth." He paused, an enigmatic smile playing upon his lips. "As I once wrote, 'it is through art, and through art only, that we can realize our perfection.'"

"Please," I implored, my heart tightening with anticipation, "tell me what you know."

"Very well, Fiona," he acquiesced, his voice low and purposeful. "Let us begin with the baroness. She was but a starry-eyed ingenue when the baron plucked her from the stage and made her his wife some twenty years ago. To rise from such humble beginnings to the pinnacle of society is no small feat, and one that she has fought tirelessly to maintain."

"Understandably," I murmured, recalling the icy elegance that defined Baroness Morton's every movement. Her desperation to preserve her status was palpable, yet it had struck me as a brittle façade, concealing a far more complex woman beneath.

"And then there is Vivienne," he continued, his eyes gleaming with relish. "She, too, had her sights set on the baron and his wealth. Yet, unlike our dear baroness, Vivienne's ambition was not tempered by any sense of loyalty or propriety. She reveled in the scandal that accompanied her rise to fame, wielding it like a weapon against the very society that sought to shun her."

"Their viciousness toward each other makes more

sense," I mused, my thoughts swirling with images of these two formidable women locked in an eternal dance of power and deceit.

"Indeed," Oscar agreed, his voice tinged with a hint of melancholy. "But it is often those who have clawed their way up from the depths who prove the most ruthless in their ascent. And in this merciless world, who can truly say what price one must pay for survival?"

"What do you mean?"

"Viv and the baroness were not social equals, but it could be argued that they are equally known and beloved by their circles. Vivienne in the *demimonde* and Clarissa in the *ton*."

"Do you think the baron was still a part of their feud?" I asked, unable to imagine the leather-faced septuagenarian at the center of this rivalry.

"I doubt it, but, as you know, Fiona, the heart is a fickle thing."

"I'm not convinced either woman was in possession of a heart, fickle or otherwise," I muttered.

"Touché!" Oscar's giggle tugged my own mouth into a smile, though my mind was still consumed by the dark allure of the stories he had shared.

"There is one more matter I would discuss with you before we part ways this evening. A delicate subject, Oscar, so forgive my boldness in broaching it."

"Boldness becomes you, my dear," he replied with a knowing smile. "Pray, continue."

"Have you ever heard of the order of the Green

Carnation?" I asked, my voice barely above a whisper. "A secret society, they say, where men of...similar proclivities might find solace in each other's intimate company."

Oscar's eyes narrowed slightly, his expression inscrutable for a moment before he answered, "Indeed, I have heard whispers of such an organization. Why do you ask?"

"Prince Albert Victor," I said, feeling a familiar knot of disquiet tighten in my stomach. "There are rumors that he was involved with this clandestine group, and possibly...with Vivienne as well."

"Ah," Oscar said, drumming his fingers thoughtfully on the arm of the chaise. "A curious connection, to be sure. But one that is not entirely implausible, given the prince's predilections and our dear Vivienne's penchant for scandal. Do you think Viv was of the sapphic variety?"

"I couldn't say," I replied, struggling to keep my voice steady as I confronted the possibility of yet another sinister alliance taking shape before my eyes. "She's most often linked to powerful men, but that could be more business than pleasure on her part. However, I cannot shake the feeling that there is more to their story than meets the eye—that something rotten lies festering at the heart of it all."

Oscar regarded me for a long moment, his gaze appraising as he weighed my words. Finally, he spoke, his tone heavy with the weight of secrets shared between old friends. "Your instincts have served you well in the past, Fiona," he said softly. "And if there is indeed some hidden truth to be unearthed from the ashes of this sordid affair, then I have no doubt your tenacity will see it brought to light. Just promise me you will treat what I have to say with discretion."

"I vow it," I breathed, eager for any insight that might guide me further down the treacherous path I had chosen.

"It is a delicate subject, Fiona, but one that I believe you shall handle with your characteristic grace and understanding."

I could not help but feel my cheeks flush at his words. Though Oscar and I had been friends for a couple of years, we did not tend to broach this subject often.

"Indeed, it is no secret to you that I prefer the company of men," he continued. "It is a truth I have long accepted, for I believe that each one of us is fabricated differently by the gods, our desires and inclinations molded by their whims.

"Yet, despite my adoration for my wife and children, I cannot abide the life I am required to live with them —the suffocating demands of society, the unyielding expectations placed upon me as a husband and father." His voice grew soft, tinged with an uncharacteristic melancholy. "The order has provided me with a refuge from the oppressive weight of convention, a place where I can be true to myself without fear or shame."

His eyes met mine, holding a depth of emotion I had never seen before. "And so, my dear Fiona, when I tell you that I *have* personally seen Prince Albert Victor among the members of the Green Carnation, know that I do not speak lightly of such matters."

My heart skipped a beat at this revelation. Could Albert Victor's connection to Vivienne be bound up in this clandestine society?

I leaned forward to share my own conspiratorial whisper. "Do you remember the strange and immediately squashed rumors that Albert Victor might have been Jack the Ripper himself?"

"I must admit," Oscar said, "the idea had crossed my mind. He is certainly worth taking a closer look at."

The shadows cast by the flickering firelight upon the vibrant tapestries seemed to whisper secrets of their own as I took in all that Oscar had shared with me. My thoughts tumbled like a swift current through my mind, carrying me toward unknown depths and murky truths.

"Oscar," I said, my voice tinged with both gratitude and steely determination, "your insights have proven invaluable. You've given me much to ponder, and your candor has not gone unnoticed, nor unappreciated."

He waved away my thanks with an elegant flick of his wrist. "It is but a simple offering, dear Fiona. As a fellow seeker of truth, it would be remiss of me not to aid you in your quest."

"Still," I insisted, "I am eternally grateful for your assistance." Rising from my seat, I felt the weight of my purpose settle around me like a cloak of iron resolve. "I shan't forget this, Oscar."

"Ah, but who could forget such a captivating conversation?" he replied, his eyes gleaming with mischief as he stretched languidly across the velvet chaise lounge. "Though I do hope our next tête-à-tête involves less murder and more merriment."

A small smile played at the corners of my mouth, despite the gravity of our discussion. "I promise nothing, but I shall endeavor to oblige."

"Good luck with your investigation, Fiona," he said, raising a hand in farewell. "And remember: 'To define is to limit.'"

"Indeed," I murmured, turning to face the door that led back into the cold night and the twisted path that lay before me. But Oscar's words echoed within me, emboldening my spirit and sharpening my senses. I was ready to embrace the darkness, to untangle the web of deceit and betrayal that ensnared those who held the power to shape our world.

As I stepped into the night, the inky sky swallowing me whole, I knew that I would not rest until the truth was revealed. For justice demanded it, and so too did the restless ghosts of my past.

Chapter Eight

As a nocturnal creature by profession, it didn't occur to me that I might be calling a bit late to accuse someone of murder.

Even in Belgravia, with its opulent façades and grandiose airs. I was a world away from the gritty streets where the Ripper's name still lurked in the dark, though one could travel between the two in the space of an hour.

A quick glance at the watch dangling from a chain on my vest told me I was, in fact, tardy for traditional calling hours. But the dark still reigned over the winter half of the year, and no self-respecting noble house would be sitting for the evening meal just yet.

The moon hung aloof in the velvet sky, a sole witness to my solitary arrival at the grand residence. The baron and baroness's address was a testament to the opulence that wealth could afford—a stone façade kissed by the ghostly caress of ivy, windows aglow with the golden warmth of gaslight, and a door as imposing as the reputation of those who dwelled within.

A chill wind whispered through the autumn foliage that flanked the garden walkway, stirring the fallen leaves into restless eddies around my skirts as I approached.

I hesitated at the hip-high gate, my hand trembling slightly as it hovered above the latch. To face the baroness alone was a daunting prospect. She was a woman woven from the same cloth as the night: dark, mysterious, veiled in elegance, but capable of unspeakable things.

"So am I," I muttered. My heart pounded in my chest, but I steeled myself against the fear that threatened to freeze me in place. There was no turning back now. I owed it to Vivienne and to Darcy to uncover the truth.

As I took a deep breath and prepared to ascend the steps to the grand entrance, I could not help but feel a sense of foreboding settle over me like a shroud.

"So are you what?" came a voice from the shadows, low and laced with an accent that was neither fully English nor entirely foreign.

I spun on my heel, a gasp escaping me before I could cage it.

Aramis Night Horse emerged from the inky tendrils of fog like a specter, his presence both startling and strangely compelling. His dark eyes held mine with an intensity that sent an unexpected shiver down my spine.

"Sweet baby Jesus, you'll be the death of me," I scolded him, scowling at his long, inky black leather coat.

"No, I won't."

Something in the solemn set of his eyes made my throat constrict, and I cleared the gathering of nerves with an irate sound. "Has anyone ever told you it's rude to move with the quietude of a reaper?"

"Given my current occupation? No," he said, the corner of his mouth tilting into a half-smile that did little to soften his fearsome mien. There was a grace to him, a deadly elegance that spoke of danger as plainly as his name.

The Blade.

He blinked down at me in his enigmatic way that made one wonder if he were amused or contemplating which of your many veins to slice first.

I eyed him with rank suspicion. "Are you following me?"

"I am not."

I should have known better than to wait for subsequent information, but I did it, more out of habit than courtesy, I'd like to think. "I refuse to believe you're merely lurking on a random corner of Belgravia and we happened upon each other."

Coincidences just didn't get *that* strange, at least not in my life.

"Jorah sent me to keep an eye on the baron and baroness," he replied, his voice low and smooth. "The question is, what brings *you* to this den of serpents?"

"Vivienne's murder, what else?"

An odd and thoroughly unexpected expression etched his features into a semblance of the man he'd once claimed to be. Husband. New father. Hunter and provider for his people.

"I knew that her ghost would stay with you after you disposed of her remains."

I regarded him carefully, noting the way the lamp-light danced across the planes of his face, casting half of it in obscurity.

"How did you know that?" In truth, I'd all but forgotten he'd been present the night of Vivienne's death. As much as a man his height, breadth, and hue might draw attention, he was excellent at obfuscation and subterfuge.

"Information is the currency of our trade, is it not?" He didn't answer my question, though there was a glimmer in his eye, a flicker of intrigue? "Might we barter here in the dark, Fiona?"

As we stood there in the dim light cast by the flickering gas lamps, I felt the ghost of something feral and intimate pass between us. It was a subtle, almost imperceptible shift in the air, like a whisper of silk sliding across bare skin.

A thrill, perhaps, at the notion of two lone wolves circling a common prey.

I tried to ignore it, focusing instead on relaying the information I had collected from Dr. Phillips and Detective Croft.

"The coroner mentioned that Vivienne's cause of death was a blow to the back of her head," I said, noting how Night Horse's eyes seemed to gleam with fascination. "That the sword was used postmortem to pin her to the ground. He also said the angle of the blow suggested the assailant might not be very tall. Perhaps closer to my height."

"Intriguing," Night Horse mused, his brow furrowing in thought as he looked down a good six inches to me. "In the interest of fairness, I'll tell you the maid, Claudia, mentioned to Jorah that Vivienne had been furious with the baroness as recently as last week. The lady had blocked Vivienne's acting company from debuting at the West End theater they initially wanted."

"Poor Claudia." I sighed heavily, feeling the weight of her circumstances melding our shared suspicions regarding the baroness. "Do you trust her as a source of information?"

"I trust no one."

I gulped at the gravitas in his tone before replying, "I meant, do you think she could have done the violence to her mistress? Or been involved? I've learned she was a rather...ardent admirer of Vivienne's, and we've all learned that sometimes obsession can blur the lines between love and hate."

Our gazes locked and we stared at each other for

several breaths, each of us reliving our worst shared moment.

My former fiancé, Aidan Fitzpatrick, had renounced our engagement and devoted himself to the church upon his return to Ireland from America. However, his decision to become a priest did not absolve him of the guilt he carried for his role in the horrific extermination of Native Americans during the age of Manifest Destiny. In fact, it only drove him into madness. Night Horse had reaped a bloody vengeance against Aidan for his actions.

But revenge always came far too late, after countless innocent lives had already been lost and forgotten in mass graves.

It was something we rarely discussed, though it always hung in the air between us.

Blunted, I think, by this strange fascination we felt for each other.

"Maybe we should combine our efforts on this," Night Horse suggested, his gaze holding mine with an intensity that made my heart race. "For the sake of expediency."

"That would be most welcome," I replied, unable to deny the sense of camaraderie flowering between us. "It seems the baroness and Vivienne were once rivals for the baron's affections."

"Jealousy is a potent motive," he murmured, leaning in as if drawn by the gravity of our discourse. "And what of Darcy? You do not believe him a suspect at all?"

"My goal is to clear his name—to cast suspicion where it rightfully belongs." The words felt heavy on my tongue, laden with an urgency that brooked no argument. "If the evidence points to Darcy, then, well..."

Then I'd have to come to terms with the fact that another of my childhood heroes had grown into a murderer.

I shook the thought away, latching on to another. "The baroness, with her stature and cunning, could well have struck the fatal blow to Vivienne's head. It was why I hesitated when you found me here on her walk. I was wondering how foolish it was of me to come here alone."

"Ah," Night Horse intoned, his interest visibly piqued. "I can think of several individuals who would have readily accompanied you."

"Can you?" I huffed. "Because everyone I can think of has already forbidden me from taking a closer look at Vivienne's death *because it's too dangerous for a woman* or some such codswallop." I realized I was applying a little too much sarcasm than the situation warranted, but I didn't care.

"They do not know that to forbid you is to send you in that very direction." Night Horse wasn't a man who often smiled, but his dark eyes glinted when he made an observation that pleased him.

For some reason, though it was not strictly a compliment, his remark pleased me, too.

Our exchange hung in the gathering mist, charged

with the electric hum of shared purpose. I was aware, then, of an undercurrent that thrummed beneath the surface of our words—a connection wrought not merely from necessity but from an unspoken recognition of each other's solitary paths.

"You mean to speak with Baroness Morton?" he asked, glancing toward the oak edifice of the door.

"That was my intention."

"Would you object to my attendance, as well?"

The chill of evening seeped through my woolen cloak as I chewed my lip, the weight of his offer sitting like a crow on my shoulder.

"Would my objection even make a difference? If I closed and locked the door against you, you'd just kick it down."

"That is not my way," he replied, that mischievous glint returning to his eye. "If the door is locked, I wait for the house to fall asleep and come in through the window. Via the drainpipe or roof. That is why Jorah is called the Hammer, and I the Blade. He is spectacle. I am shadow."

It took me three attempts to successfully swallow. "Well, that's very nice for you, but you're right that it won't be easy to get her to talk with you in the room being so...well, tall, with your muscles, and—and you're menacing."

His dark brow arched. "I shall assume the guise of your manservant—silent, unobtrusive. So utterly foreign as to not even be considered a human."

"You cannot pass as a *servant*," I insisted before barking out a laugh brought on by the lunacy of the idea.

"My livery not up to snuff?" He motioned to his impeccable shirt, cravat, and trousers beneath the slick black of his overcoat. "Perhaps it is my manner that offends? Or still yet, my color?"

I couldn't swallow around a tongue dry as the Sahara, feeling a pang of remorse and resentment that his native appearance should be considered sinister. When, indeed, it was the loveliest thing about him.

"I'll thank you not to tease," I spat. "You very well know you can't pass as the sort of man who bows to the whim of others. Not for recompense or any fathomable reason. Your gaze is too direct to be deferential to a master. You're too braw and broad to be considered a footman or valet. You're too, I don't know...regal and well appointed for a stable master but not dandy enough for a solicitor or a clerk, so I don't see how—"

It was his hand on my folded forearm that interrupted me before he even opened his mouth to say a word, a ghost of a true smile playing at the corners of his lips. "Trust me. This is a gambit I often apply with Jorah. Tell the baroness I am your manservant. She will draw her own conclusions from there, which you can validate. It will help you to build rapport."

I blinked up at him, open-mouthed, for several seconds before turning on my heel and marching up the steps.

Upon my ringing the bell, a footman opened the door then led us to the baroness's private parlor without delay and announced us as "Miss Fiona Mahoney and guest."

The opulence was immediately suffocating. Gilded mirrors reflected our figures in endless repetition, while lush velvet curtains held the world at bay.

The parlor was bathed in a soft, golden light from the candles flickering on every surface, casting shadows that danced upon the rich tapestries lining the walls. The air was heavy with the scent of roses, their red petals strewn carelessly across the polished wooden sideboard.

The baroness herself was an image of haughty elegance, reclining amidst settee pillows. Her flawless porcelain skin was complemented by her perfectly coiffed raven hair, while her ice-blue eyes seemed to pierce through me as she appraised my entrance.

We weren't invited to sit. In fact, she said nothing as we approached quietly on lush carpets.

"Good evening, baroness," I said, my voice steady despite the unease coiling within me. "I don't know if you remember, but we met briefly at the Velvet Glove the night of Vivienne Bloomfield-Smythe's death. I have been engaged by Mr. Darcy O'Dowd to look into the unfortunate matter of Vivienne's murder. I thought it prudent to seek a woman's perspective, as they are often overlooked in such investigations, and since you and Vivienne were acquainted for so long—"

"You heard that Vivienne and I hated each other for a long time, so you've come to see if I'm a viable scapegoat for your countryman's crimes." As if to underscore her villainy, she picked up a sleek ginger cat that wound its way into her skirts and settled it on her lap.

Well, I'd give the woman one thing: she was smarter than she looked. "That isn't—"

"*You're* an investigator? Irish. A woman. My, how times have changed..." the baroness drawled, her gaze drifting over to Night Horse as she stroked the purring predator in her lap. "And what is this? Does it speak English?"

"*He* is my manservant," I explained, bristling on Night Horse's behalf. He caught my eye and gave a brief nod, complicit in our ruse. "He does not speak English well, but he understands enough to earn his keep."

"Does he, now?" A glimmer of impishness lit her eyes as she leaned forward, lowering her voice to a tone silkier than the shawl draped across her shoulders. "Does he service you in all the ways a woman might require?"

I felt the color rise to my cheeks, but I kept my response ambiguous, my words seasoned with just enough suggestion to stoke her curiosity. "He fulfills his duties most satisfactorily."

A chuckle escaped her lips, rich and velvety, as she reclined against the cushions. Night Horse remained stoic beside me, though the faintest twitch of his lips indicated his amusement.

"Indeed," the baroness breathed out, her eyes still fixed on my silent companion. "One must appreciate a man who can satisfy the demands of *any* position required."

Her words hung in the room, laced with double entendre, as I forced myself to focus on the task at hand, unwilling to allow her to manipulate the conversation. Our exchange was a dance of shadows and suggestion, and I knew then that extracting the truth from the baroness would be like plucking thorns from a rose —delicate, dangerous, and likely to draw blood.

"Baroness," I began, attempting to steer the conversation back to the matter at hand. "I'll admit I understood that you and Vivienne were rivals for the baron's affections some twenty years ago."

"And you think it took me two decades to reap my revenge?" She cackled so sharply, the cat scampered from her lap in a startle. "For what, darling? I won. The baron has held me as his muse all this time, indulging my every whim. What possible grudge could I hold against Viv? She's been forced to sing for her supper, and there are fewer and fewer men to foot the bill at her age."

She said this as if unaware she'd aged right alongside Vivienne.

Aged rather well, all told.

"Perhaps you could share your thoughts on some of the other individuals involved?" I pressed, watching her closely.

She made a huffing sound in the back of her throat and reached for a silver case on the table at her elbow, extracting a cigarette and an ornate box of matches. "Anything I would tell you is pure speculation, of course. I know nothing but rumors."

"Rumors often have seeds of truth," I replied, watching as her gaze flitted toward the window, where the firelight cast shadows long and deceitful across the pale carpets.

"Ah, but which truths?" The baroness's voice was a melody of insinuation. "Miss Mahoney. It is true that many in my circle have secrets they'd rather keep hidden. I do not want to be considered the leak in the ship."

"Of course," I acquiesced, noting her evasiveness. "Nonetheless, any information you might provide could help bring Vivienne's killer to justice... I would treat it with the utmost discretion."

"Very well." The baroness seemed to weigh her words carefully before continuing. "As you may know, Jorah and Vivienne had a tumultuous affair some seven or so years past, which ended quite poorly. There's word she let something slip that sent the Syndicate against Jorah and took him no small amount of work to unravel."

I'd heard she'd stolen from him, but nothing about imperiling his place in the criminal enterprise. Of course, Jorah would never implicate himself, and I certainly didn't want to believe he'd hire me if I'd uncover enough clues to investigate him.

Surely he believed in my skills better than that.

The baroness wasn't finished with her thought. "To be fair, Vivienne has been connected to a swath of undesirable men. Oswald Drumft, for example... A man of ruthless ambition and no morals. She's been rumored to have been kept and shared by half the House of Hapsburg and twice as many Saxe-Coburgs, not to mention our own dear Albert Victor, though one must be careful when speaking of such matters, Miss Mahoney. Royalty is not to be trifled with."

"Indeed," I agreed, sensing that she would say no more on the subject. "But one must also acknowledge that power can be a dangerous weapon in the wrong hands."

"Which is why I shall steer clear of the entire affair, and you would too if you know what is good for you."

At that, Night Horse stepped forward, "Are you threatening her?" he asked, his voice as smooth as silk.

"I'm warning her," she replied, not seeming surprised in the least to hear him speak perfect English. "People who investigate the royal family often find themselves imprisoned...or worse." She drew a line over her throat with a sharply pointed nail on her index finger.

As our conversation drew to a close, I found myself increasingly unsettled by the baroness's elusive demeanor. She had skillfully deflected my inquiries, casting suspicion on each potential suspect without implicating herself. Yet something in her bearing, an unspoken tension that lay beneath her elegant façade, told me that she was probably not to blame for Vivienne's murder.

But nor was she innocent.

"Before I take my leave, baroness, might I ask if you've ever heard of an organization known as the Order of the Green Carnation?"

For the first time, her composure faltered, the ghost of a frown creasing her flawless brow. "I can't say that I have," she responded, her voice clipped, the warmth of our earlier exchange chilled by suspicion.

"Curious," I murmured, my mind working furiously to stitch together the disjointed tapestry of her defenses. "It is said to be quite exclusive."

"Many things in London are," she retorted, rising to her full height, her elegance unmarred by the hint of steel in her tone. "Now, if you'll excuse me, I have other engagements to attend to."

"Of course, baroness," I said, bowing my head slightly. "Your insights have been most enlightening."

As we withdrew from the parlor, I felt the weight of her gaze upon us, heavy and calculating. In the silence that followed, I knew that the dance was far from over, and that the baroness, like all great predators, was most dangerous when cornered.

Night Horse trailed behind me, his silent footsteps testament to a lifetime honed in stealth. As we emerged into the dimly lit corridor, I sighed. "I can't help but feel we're no closer to the truth than when we began."

"Perhaps not," he murmured, his voice low and thoughtful, "but at least we have more pieces to the puzzle. It's up to us to fit them together."

My eyes narrowed as we exited the grand residence and descended the elegant steps onto the cobblestone street. The somber sky above mirrored my brooding thoughts, casting shadows that seemed to reflect the darkness of the secrets surrounding Vivienne's murder.

"I sense you have pieces I do not," I told him honestly.

To my astonishment, he nodded. "The baron and Herr Drumft are each other's alibis for the time of the murder," he said. "She could be covering for her husband, who seems to have slipped out of the country."

I tossed my head with what I feared was an equine snort. "Baron Morton and Oswald J. Drumft? That duo reeks of contrivance."

"Agreed," Night Horse replied, his eyes narrowing as he glanced over my shoulder a second before yanking me into the shadows and covering my yelp of surprise with his palm.

With his free arm around my waist, he crushed me against his body, and I froze, paralyzed like a rabbit caught in a snare.

A warm snare made of lengthy, lithe sinew and hard male muscle.

"Look." Night Horse pointed me in the direction of the baroness's gate.

There, approaching the Morton residence with the assured stride of a man who owned the pavement beneath his feet, was Oswald J. Drumft. His top hat sat at a rakish angle, and there was an arrogance to his posture that suggested a life unaccustomed to being contradicted.

"If we'd lingered any longer, we'd have had to talk to the blighter," I whispered, watching the butler open the door with a bow that bordered on obsequious. "Look at the lout. Carries himself as if he's above the law."

"Or believes he can bend it to his will," Night Horse murmured back.

"Perhaps we should—" My suggestion was cut short by the sight of the butler whispering something into Drumft's ear. Whatever the words exchanged, they elicited a sharp nod from the Prussian before he disappeared within the house, like a wolf slinking into his den.

"Wait to see how long he visits the baroness and where he's headed after?" Night Horse asked.

"You took the words right out of my mouth," I said. "Now, if you'll unhand me..."

Surprisingly, he did.

Ensconced in the dense shadows of a London evening, Night Horse and I remained statuesque, our breaths mingling with the mist that rose from the cobblestones. The gas lamps cast an ethereal glow on the street, their flickering light throwing elongated silhouettes against the walls of the baroness's residence.

"Patience is a virtue, but it's not one of mine," I murmured, my voice barely more than a wisp in the cool air. I had my eyes trained on the heavy oak door of the house, willing it to open and reveal its secrets.

"Yet here you are, a study in perseverance," Night Horse replied, his proximity a tangible thing in the dark —comforting and unsettling all at once.

His nearness was indeed pleasant, a fact I allowed myself to acknowledge only in the privacy of my own mind. The warmth of him seeped into me, chasing away the chill that clung to my bones. It was an unexpected solace in the midst of our grim vigil.

"Drumft's been in there too long for a simple courtesy call," I noted, the detective within me growing anxious.

"Or just long enough for a conspiratorial one," he countered softly, his keen gaze never leaving the door.

We stood in silence, the minutes stretching taut between us. Then, as if summoned by our collective will, the door to the baroness's house swung open. Drumft emerged, his posture stiff, his head swiveling this way and that with furtive glances that spoke of inner turmoil.

I observed the Prussian man exiting the residence, his gait unnaturally brisk, betraying the confident façade he had exuded earlier. He paused at the top of the steps, pulling out a pocket watch, and its metallic surface glinted beneath the moonlight. His fingers drummed impatiently upon its engraved casing, as if time itself were conspiring against him.

"Look at his hands," I whispered, my breath catching in my throat as I noted the way they tremored ever so slightly. Guilt? Fear? Or simply the weight of whatever secrets he carried? "Something isn't right."

Night Horse inclined his head, analyzing Drumft's every movement with the precision of a predator stalking its prey. "He is not satisfied with the outcome of whatever happened in there."

As Drumft strode down the walkway, he unconsciously patted his coat pocket, ensuring whatever he'd placed was still there.

"Did you see that? What could it be?" I whispered, my pulse quickening with the implication of concealed evidence.

"Could be nothing," Night Horse replied, his voice a low rumble next to my ear. "Could be everything,"

I tugged against his grip to almost no avail. "Let's follow. We cannot let him slip away."

Night Horse's dark eyes flashed with determination, and his voice echoed the urgency I felt. "You must promise to keep me between your body and his at all times."

"Understood," I said. And I meant it, too. I'd no pressing need to be anywhere near Oswald Drumft, his tiny hands, or his enormous ego.

As we began our pursuit, I couldn't help but be

acutely aware of Night Horse's presence beside me—the quiet cadence of his footsteps, the heat radiating from his body as he moved effortlessly through the darkness. It was a comfort, knowing that he was there, despite the dangerous path we now embarked upon.

Drumft's silhouette loomed ahead, his gait brisk and purposeful—a shadow amongst shadows. Night Horse and I trailed behind, our steps muffled by the dampness, moving like wraiths determined to unearth what lay beneath the veil of night and deceit.

"This Dublin Destroyer..." Night Horse murmured from my side. "I've noticed your interactions with the fighter. Do you...have feelings for him?"

My eyes remained fixed on Drumft's retreating figure, but my mind raced. Was it so obvious? "No," I replied, truthfully. "He's like a brother to me. Besides, he's just lost his fiancée. I couldn't possibly entertain such thoughts."

"Then why are you going to such lengths to help him?" he asked, his voice soft yet insistent.

"Because I believe in justice," I answered, the words tasting bitter on my tongue. "Darcy is innocent, and it's my duty to find the real killer. For old times' sake, if nothing else."

Night Horse nodded, accepting my explanation without further inquiry. The silence that followed was heavy with unspoken thoughts and shared conviction. We continued our pursuit, melding into the shadows as we closed in on our quarry.

As we trailed Drumft through the dark alleys and gaslit streets, I couldn't help but wonder what secrets he held. What role had he played in Vivienne's murder? And how would this tangled web of lies and deceit unravel in the end?

The cityscape around us grew darker, more ominous, as we ventured deeper into the heart of London. Gas lamps cast eerie shadows on the brick walls, and the distant echoes of carriages and laughter gave way to the sound of raindrops splattering against the ground. It was as if we had entered a realm of secrets and shadows, where nothing was as it seemed.

"Look, there," Night Horse murmured, nodding toward a narrow alleyway where Drumft had come to an abrupt halt. Checking a notepad from his pocket, he verified the address before slipping inside a nondescript building, closing the door behind him with a soft click.

"Shall we follow?" I asked, my pulse quickening at the prospect of uncovering yet another layer of intrigue.

"Wait," Night Horse instructed me, holding up a hand to stall my advance. "We must be cautious."

His intensity sent a thrill down my spine, igniting within me a fierce determination to see this quest through to its bitter end. Together, we approached the building with catlike stealth, our eyes adjusting to the gloom as we peered through a crack in the door.

"Remember. Keep me between you and anyone else," Night Horse whispered, his breath warm on my cheek. "Even if they seem safe."

"I will," I replied, swallowing my apprehension as we prepared to step into the unknown.

With that, Night Horse pushed open the door just enough for us to slip inside, and we were immediately plunged into a world of shadows.

Chapter Nine

❧

The sound of battle assaulted us, echoing in fractals from down a dark hall.

The moment we slipped through the creaking door, the stench of mildew, men, and liniment assaulted my senses. A cacophony of grunts and the thud of leather against flesh filled the dimly lit space. A gymnasium, cavernous and echoing with pugilistic combatants locked in their dance of violence. The atmosphere was thick, heavy—laden with the scent of sweat and iron resolve.

We melded with the shadows, our presence cloaked by a discreet alcove that offered an unobstructed view of the gym's gritty interior.

"By the saints," I muttered, tugging at the collar of my blouse, which all at once seemed too tight as I took in the fighters' near-naked torsos gleaming with perspiration, muscles straining and contracting with every calculated blow. The sheer dedication etched into the grimaces of these pugilists spoke volumes of their commitment to the brutal ballet of fisticuffs. They fought like men possessed, driven by some unfathomable inner demon, or perhaps the simple promise of coin and glory.

"Look at them," I breathed, unable to pull my eyes away. "They're completely consumed by their craft."

"Much like you are with yours," Night Horse observed, his tone unreadable.

"Except I don't bare my soul, my skin—or anything else, for that matter—for the world to see," I countered, though I couldn't deny the parallel. My quest for justice was much like a fight, relentless, exhausting, often painful and brutal.

"You touch what most cannot bring themselves to look at. Lives like ours do not call for us to seek a spectacle," he conceded, a flash of a smirk discernible even in the shadowed space. "But you cannot mask the fire in you, Fiona Mahoney. It burns as bright as any here."

To hide my discomfiture at his words, I swept my gaze across the room, taking in the half-naked forms of the fighters, muscles coiling and flexing with each deliberate movement. The raw power on display, unfettered by the decorum of society's dress, stirred something primal within me—a recognition of the struggle between man and his baser nature.

"Look," Night Horse murmured, his voice barely

above the resonance of leather against flesh. "The Prussian snake slithers into the pit."

Oswald J. Drumft, in all his corpulent menace, breached the threshold of the gymnasium. His eyes, sharp as flint, scanned the room before settling on his quarry, a large, bald fighter in the far corner with a handler the size of a lamppost.

"Henry 'the London Lion' Lewis," Night Horse said, answering the question before I had the chance to ask it. "Darcy's opponent for Sunday's match."

Drumft exchanged not threats or pleasantries, but an envelope sealed with an umbral insignia with Lewis's manager—a man to whom shadows seemed to cling like tendrils of suspicion.

"I thought Drumft was investing heavily with Jorah into Darcy's victory," I said.

"As did we all."

"Then...why put money on the opposition?" I asked, unable to contain my curiosity any longer.

"Most likely it's not a bet but a bribe," Night Horse replied, narrowing his eyes in thought. "The question is, for what purpose? To ensure victory, or defeat?"

"Surely *this* has nothing to do with Vivienne's murder," I whispered, my gaze not leaving Drumft's clandestine conversation. "That envelope wasn't large enough to contain a sufficient sum for a life."

Night Horse made a wry sound in the back of his throat. "Surely *you're* not so naïve as that."

"I heartily beg your pardon?" I huffed, scowling up at him. "I hardly think—"

"Anywhere there is competition between men, there will be murder," he stated with a finality that rankled my skin.

"Competition? That's ridiculous. This is a game. A folly. A—"

"Life is a game, Fiona, survival the prize. It is why the path to alpha predator is so blood-soaked and brutal. And humans, for some unfathomable reason, stand at the top of it all. The best killers this world has yet seen. And we will find any reason to do it, even one so stupid as nicked pride. So do not ascribe men the nobility of women. You will be forever disappointed."

I stared at him for a moment, forgetting where we were. What we were doing. I couldn't think of a thing to say, so I opened my mouth and let the first thing that slipped out be my response. "You might be the only honest man I know, Aramis Night Horse."

His response was an enigmatic nod. I didn't know if he agreed, unburdened by the false modesty of my people, or if he was too polite to disabuse me of the notion. Either way, we said nothing else on the matter.

Instead, Night Horse brought the conversation back to the vocation at hand. "Men like Drumft, they've never known the grave's embrace, the stench of war. To them, this—money, power—is their battlefield. And they'll slay as mercilessly as any soldier to keep their coffers full."

I felt a sick twist in my gut, the idea that Vivienne's life—a woman of such vivacity and cunning—could have been snuffed out over a pittance or pride at a boxing match was abhorrent.

My heart quickened as I considered the implications. A bribe to sway the match, to tarnish the reputation of one and elevate another?

"It figures Drumft's up to his elbows in muck," I said, the words tasting of ash and resolve. "We must tread carefully. For if he's willing to tamper with the integrity of a fight, who knows what else he's capable of?"

"Men have long spilled blood over less," Night Horse continued, his eyes like chips of obsidian in the gloom, reflecting the brutality before us. "Their pride, their legacy—gambling offers them a battlefield without the inconvenience of war. It's all about conquest, be it land, coin, or another man's will."

His words wove a tapestry of dark insight, a world where survival was not just against nature but against the mediocrity that threatened to render one insignificant. My own past whispered to me then, a grim reminder that violence was as much a part of me as the very blood coursing through my veins.

Drumft adjusted his lapels as if to signal the meeting was over, and took his leave with a dramatic whorl of his cloak.

Night Horse's eyes met mine, a silent pact forged in the crucible of shared determination. We would unravel this mystery, brick by sordid brick, until the edifice of lies crumbled beneath the weight of truth.

"Keep your wits sharp," he murmured as we melded into the evening's gloom. "Drumft is a serpent that will elude you if you let him."

"Let him slither," I breathed, feeling the weight of the city's oppressive darkness settle on my shoulders. "We are the hawk, and hawks have keen eyes indeed."

"You are a raven," Night Horse corrected me.

"A raven?" I wrinkled my nose. "Aren't they sinister portents of death?"

"To these people, not to mine." He shrugged. "Ravens most often appear after a death has occurred and are an important part of the death cycle. They are loyal. Intelligent. Communicative. Resourceful." He looked down at me for a moment, and I could imagine he forgot about the task at hand when he gazed at me like that.

I certainly did.

"They're beautiful," he said before turning to lead us back out into the dark.

I'd admit to finding it thrilling, walking as a phantom in Night Horse's realm. Every step we took was measured, every breath controlled, as we slipped unseen into the murky night. Our quarry moved ahead, unaware of the specters at his heels, each footfall leading us deeper into an abyss of corruption and secrets.

The streets of London had become a treacherous

labyrinth, each turn more menacing than the last. We followed Drumft's shadowed form, our footsteps echoing softly against the cobblestones.

The relative quiet was shattered by a sudden explosion of chaos and aggression. Two monstrous figures emerged from the shadows of an alleyway, their intentions glimmering with the malice in their eyes.

A startled cry tore from my lips as instinct propelled me backward.

But Aramis Night Horse—part man, part primal force—met the ambush with a fearsome grace.

His fist struck first, a sound blow to the larger assailant's jaw that snapped the brute's head back with a crack. The man staggered, but Night Horse was relentless, his movements a dark ballet choreographed to the rhythm of survival. Another vicious punch crunched into cartilage; a nose flattened with brutal efficiency.

"Behind you!" I warned, balling my own hands into fists.

But Night Horse needed no assistance. He spun and caught the second attacker's arm mid-swing. There was a grotesque symphony of snapping tendons and breaking bone as he twisted sharply, rendering the limb useless. The man howled, a guttural cry that echoed through the foggy air, his face contorted in agony.

"Run to your master!" Night Horse growled, his voice a harbinger of doom. The injured brute didn't hesitate—with a whimper, he fled past us, past Oswald Drumft, who'd turned to play spectator to the carnage.

"Remember this mercy," Night Horse called to Drumft, a dark promise lacing his tone. "Your next lackeys won't be so fortunate."

I shivered, not from the cold, but from the deadly calm in Night Horse's eyes as he turned to survey the scene. The remaining brute lay crumpled on the ground, gasping through shattered teeth.

The fog of the London night seemed to coil tighter around us as Night Horse and I approached the imposing figure of Oswald J. Drumft. The Prussian's eyes, cold and calculating, flicked between us with the measured disdain of a man who believed himself untouchable.

"Roth's minions, are you? Only a Jew would send a savage and an Irish whore to do his dirty work," Drumft spat, apparently deciding to go on the offensive after being caught misbehaving.

"Seems his distrust is warranted," I volleyed back. I'd been raised with too many brothers to allow him to get away with such childish behavior, and knew that rising to the occasion would invite more abuse. "Tell me, Herr Drumft, are you paying Mr. Lewis to throw the fight or to win it by some cheeky swindle? All of London will want to know."

His countenance remained as impassive as a marble bust, yet within those cold eyes, I discerned the flicker of something feral. "Miss Mahoney," he replied, his voice thick with scorn. "You presume to accuse me with nothing but suppositions and whispers?"

"Accuse you? No." I tilted my head, feigning overex-aggerated innocence. "We both saw the envelope change hands."

"The envelope will be easy enough for me to take from Lewis and his manager," Night Horse threatened. "What *won't* be easy, *for you*, is explaining to Mr. Roth why you are playing both sides of this match."

I had to give him credit—though his skin paled, Drumft's lip curled into a sneer. "I don't need to explain myself to anyone," he blustered. "This is business, Miss Mahoney. A realm where predators thrive, and the likes of you are devoured. Look at what happened to poor Miss Bloomfield."

The way he said her name grated against my skin. It felt less like a mispronunciation, and more like a dese-cration.

"Jorah will hear of this business," Night Horse inter-jected, his tone deceptively calm.

"I do not see why he will care." Drumft gave an infu-riating shrug. "Nothing that happened here tonight will affect his outcome. He stands to make as much money as I will. If he has follow-up questions, I suggest he seeks me out himself, as I do not work with interme-diaries."

He tipped his hat, and something inside of me snapped. "What about Vivienne?" I demanded. "Your contempt for her—"

"Is no secret," Drumft replied, irate. His arrogance was a palpable force, as if he could will us into nonexistence with sheer disdain. "But do not mistake my contempt for guilt. Everyone hated Vivienne, but as you might have noticed, much like Roth, I pay others to do my wet work."

Which was why I didn't find his alibi provided by the baron compelling in the least.

"Yet here you are under the cloak of night. An envelope with an umbral seal changes hands, and suddenly one cannot help but speculate."

"If you want to speculate about a manager, look to your own. Tunstall is worthy of your surveillance, not I," Drumft retorted with a dismissive wave of his hand. "I wager on both fighters. One openly, the other in shadow. That is my affair."

"Indeed, it is," I conceded, locking gazes with him. "But perhaps you might enlighten us as to why Mr. Tunstall should draw our attention instead?"

Drumft's mouth twisted into a grimace of distaste. "He's been skulking about with secrets that would make the devil himself blush. Secrets a man ought never to have."

"Secrets that might lead to murder?" I prodded, arching an eyebrow.

"Perhaps." Drumft stepped closer, his breath a foul whisper against my cheek. "They're secrets I would kill to keep. Either way, they're buried deep. And I would tread warily, Miss Mahoney."

"Are you threatening her?" Night Horse took a step forward, driving Drumft to mirror the motion in retreat.

"Your insinuations are as tiresome as they are base-less." Drumft's lip curled. "I wager on fighters—it's a pastime, nothing more."

"Both fighters?" Night Horse asked, the moonlight casting deep shadows across his chiseled features. "That seems a rather duplicitous strategy."

"Life is a game of chances, Mr. Night Horse. Betting on both simply improves the odds." Drumft shrugged, his arrogance as heavy as the velvet cloak draped over his shoulders. "A man doesn't become as successful as I am by taking unnecessary risks. Which leads me back to George Tunstall. That man harbors more secrets than the catacombs of Paris. I'm telling you, uncover them and you will find your killer."

"Is that an admission of innocence or a deflection of guilt?" I challenged, though something in Drumft's demeanor suggested his cruel nature might not extend to murder. He was a serpent, certainly, but perhaps not our viper.

"Believe what you will, Miss Mahoney," he said. "It's of no consequence to me. Now, if you'll excuse me, I have matters to attend that do not involve entertaining the wild theories of an Irish charwoman and her savage companion." The corner of his mouth twitched into a semblance of a smile, devoid of warmth. "My security detail will be thickened, tripled if need be. They'll have orders—shoot first, inquire later."

With a derisive snort, Drumft turned his back to us,

signaling that our audience had concluded. But the air remained thick with the scent of suspicion and the unspoken threats that hung between us like the mist that shrouded our shoes.

"He could be surrounded by legions," Night Horse murmured. "I'd still want to spill his blood."

"Indeed," I replied, my mind churning with plans and possibilities. But even as we drifted in the opposite direction, a shiver of foreboding traced down my spine, the whispered caress of the unseen and the unheard—a harbinger of the darkness that lay ahead.

Chapter Ten

❖

A cold brush against my cheek roused me from a restless slumber, the remnants of a nightmare clinging like cobwebs to my consciousness.

My eyes slammed open to the sight of Aunt Nola looming over me, her silhouette a wraith in the moonlit chamber.

"Child," she whispered, the urgency in her voice cutting through the silence like a knife. "The Queen of Swords... She beckons." Her thin frame was draped in flowing black fabric that clung to her bony shoulders. An intricate lace veil obscured her face, its webbed pattern casting shadows across her hollow cheeks.

I sat up, the mattress creaking beneath me, and rubbed the sleep from my eyes. The card was thrust before my face again, its image stark and forbidding. Aunt Nola stood there, a fragile figure cloaked in black, her red hair a wild mane that seemed almost aflame in the pale light. The lace veil draped over her face did little to hide the fervor in her green eyes, or the tremble in her outstretched hand.

I suppressed a groan. *Not again.* My father's elder sister's episodes of madness came on suddenly, without warning. One moment she could be lucid, even warm, the next, lost in a world of spirits and omens only she could see.

"Look at her, Fiona," she implored. "She warns us!"

Her words hung heavy in the air, a portent wrapped in the mad echoes of her mind. Nola's schizophrenia was a living, breathing entity in our home; it danced in her gaze and spoke in cryptic tongues through her lips. Yet, despite the illness that ravaged her reason, there was an unnerving truth to her delusions—a prophecy entwined with madness.

"Warns us of what, Aunt?" I asked, my voice steady despite the chill that crept up my spine.

"Betrayal...death," she whispered, caressing the edges of the tarot card as if it were a lover. "The Queen of Swords is a harbinger. She cuts through deceit, yes, but her blade is double-edged." Her gaze pierced into mine, seeking understanding—or perhaps validation for the dark omens she read in the cards.

"Death has been our constant companion of late," I replied, the weight of London's sins heavy on my shoulders. "And deceit is the currency of this city's soul."

I gritted my teeth, fighting back my frustration.

Nola meant well, even in her madness. But her cryptic ramblings often left me more confused than enlightened.

"Danger lurks in your path. The Queen of Swords is a warning. When she is angry, she will cut down all in her path."

"What is she angry about?" I asked gently. "Have I done something to upset her?"

Nola's veiled face turned toward me, her eyes flashing in the darkness. "You tread dangerous ground, Fiona. Your quest for truth disturbs restless souls. Do not look in the queen's direction. That way lies madness."

I shuddered despite myself. When Nola spoke like this, in riddles laced with warning, it was hard not to feel a prickle of unease.

But I could not stop now. Too many unanswered questions remained. Vivienne's murder, Jack the Ripper's identity, the web of lies and secrets ensnaring those I thought I knew... I had to keep digging, no matter the risk.

Drawing my blanket close, I chose my next words carefully. "I understand, Aunt Nola. I will be cautious."

She searched my face with feverish eyes, as if trying to ascertain the truth of my words. At last, she gave a jerky nod. Clutching the Queen of Swords to her breast, she scurried from the room in a swirl of black fabric.

I released a shaky breath. Sleep would not return

easily tonight. I lay awake staring at the ceiling, my thoughts churning like the dark waters of the Thames.

Aunt Nola's warning echoed in my mind. I was no follower of faith or tarot, but I couldn't stop thinking on it.

"Queen of Swords," I whispered to myself. "Cuts through deception, and those who cross her path risk her wrath."

I had no doubt the fair Vivienne could embody such ruthlessness if crossed.

As could our actual monarch, Queen Victoria.

Strange that she would present herself to someone who thought nothing of her at all.

Stranger still that I was lending those silly cards any credence.

And yet... Hadn't I only just discussed Albert Victor with Croft? His position as the Duke of Clarence afforded him immense privilege and protection. I shuddered to imagine the wrath that could be brought down upon me for prying into his affairs.

The whispers of his possible involvement in Mary Kelly's murder had haunted me since that fateful day when Vivienne Bloomfield-Smythe's lifeless body had been found. It was my determination to bring justice for my dear friend that had led me down this twisted path, but I couldn't deny the dread that now coiled within me. If the Queen of Swords represented the consequences of investigating Albert Victor, then her wrath was not something to be taken lightly.

Yet the prince was but one player in this mystery. Jorah, Tunstall, the baroness, Claudia, even Darcy—all were tangled in Vivienne's web of secrets. And I could not forget the specter of Jack the Ripper, who I *knew* still lurked in London's shadows.

THE MORNING SUN had barely begun to streak the sky with crimson when I found myself standing before the modest house where Night Horse had informed me that Claudia, Vivienne's maid, was staying with a relative. A hand-painted sign advertised the cluttered stoop as "The Harringtons."

The quiet of Lambeth High street masked the turmoil within me, my determination at odds with the unease that gnawed at my insides. I rapped sharply on the door, and it was opened by a tired-looking woman I took to be the cousin. She regarded me warily.

"Good morning. I've come to call upon Claudia," I said briskly. "It concerns her late mistress."

The woman's eyes widened in understanding, and she ushered me inside. "Please wait here a moment."

I stood in the narrow foyer, listening to her footsteps fade down the hall. Then came the creak of a door opening, the murmur of voices.

After a few minutes Claudia appeared, clad in a rumpled black dress, her eyes rimmed red. She looked as if she had not slept in days. Wordlessly she led me to the kitchen, where we could speak privately. Her hair, once neatly coiled atop her head, now hung in loose tendrils around her sallow cheeks. Her grief clung to her like a shroud, making her seem even more fragile than she already was.

"Miss Mahoney," she whispered, her voice trembling. "What brings you here so early?"

"Forgive the intrusion, but I have some questions about Vivienne," I said softly, trying to mask the urgency of my mission beneath a veil of sympathy. "I've been asked to assist with the inquiry into her death." I knew I made it sound more official than it actually was, but…needs must.

"Vivienne meant the world to me," she confessed, fresh tears welling up in her eyes. "I would have done anything for her."

"Which is precisely why I've come to you, Claudia," I said, leaning forward. "I believe there are still secrets surrounding Vivienne's murder, and I need your help to uncover them."

"Secrets?" she echoed, her eyes widening with a mix of fear and curiosity. "What more could there be to discover? She's already gone."

"Her past, Claudia. There are still unanswered questions about her past, and I believe the answers may lie in her private scheduling diary?"

"Her diary?" She hesitated, twisting her fingers in her lap. "I thought the inspectors looked at it already."

"Yes, I checked with the constable collecting the

evidence and was told it's missing from her effects... Please, Claudia," I implored, my voice soft but insistent as I reached across the table and took her rough hands in mine. "Vivienne deserves justice, and we must do everything we can to ensure it is served."

A moment of silence hung between us, fraught with tension and uncertainty. Finally, Claudia let out a shaky breath and nodded.

"All right," she whispered, her voice barely audible. "But you must promise me that whatever you find will be used only to bring justice to Vivienne. Not to tarnish her memory."

"I promise," I vowed solemnly, doing my best not to give away my triumph that this hunch had borne fruit.

Her face crumpled. "Oh, miss, I would do anything for my lady. She was so very good to me..." Her voice broke off in a sob as she fled the room.

If Claudia truly thought so, I was not the one to disabuse her of the notion, but I'd not seen Vivienne treat her well at all.

Upon her return, Claudia was carrying a box rather than a book, which she settled on the table with a heavy clunk. "I save all our keepsakes in here," she huffed, lifting the lid as if the knotted pine held the holy grail.

My stomach roiled as she touched the treasures within.

First, she uncovered a lock of gold hair wrapped in a faded ribbon, then an old, tarnished tooth with a hole drilled through it. "Vivienne always had a weakness for sweets," Claudia explained, as if it were the most natural thing in the world.

It took everything inside of me to hide my revulsion before, finally, she gently laid out some obvious costume jewelry and then set a worn leather diary beside the glittering "jewels."

Yes, this obsession ran deep indeed. I laid a gentle hand on her arm, treating her as I might treat Aunt Nola. "I know this is difficult. But think how it would honor Vivienne's memory to see justice done."

At last, the pages of Vivienne's private scheduling diary lay open before me, like the petals of a dark flower. I could feel the weight of Claudia's gaze heavy upon me as I carefully turned each fragile page, brushing my fingers over the inked words that revealed the hidden corners of Vivienne's life.

"Here," I murmured, pausing at an entry that seemed to leap from the page and demand my attention. "Not a year ago she attended a voyage to the Mediterranean...on a private island owned by Geoffry Prescott, the Earl of Southaven and a rake of some repute."

"He couldn't have done her in." Claudia waved the name away like a bad wind.

"Why not?" I pressed.

"Because he's been feeding the fishes since before Christmas."

I couldn't say his death was strange, having never

met the earl, but it certainly added to the body count surrounding Vivienne.

"How did he die?" I asked.

"Can't remember." Claudia wrinkled her impish nose, shrugging. "Think it was an accident, but no one much misses him. Especially the girls in his employ, handsy bugger."

I knew the type.

"So Prince Albert Victor, the Duke of Clarence and second in line to the throne after the Prince of Wales, and Vivienne were vacationing on this island not ten months ago?"

"Yes, but I can't think of a time they ever met."

"Was Darcy among them?"

I breathed a sigh of relief when she shook her head.

"Drumft?" I pressed, to the same effect. "Jorah? The Baron or Baroness Morton?"

"Not this time, but they'd been before." Taking the book from me, Claudia flipped back and back to the summer, showing me when Vivienne had also attended a summer fete at the island alongside the baron and baroness. "I remember they attended because she made me demand the staff that she sit far away from them."

So after twenty years, Vivienne had climbed high enough on the social ladder to attend the same events as her rival from youth.

Was I reaching too far afield in order to save Darcy from his own guilt, or me from having to investigate a royal in a manner that could see me dead faster than soliciting Jack the Ripper for sex in Whitechapel on an October evening?

"What do you think of Darcy?" I asked. "You can be frank with me. I'm fond of him, but I want to find out the truth."

The look she flashed me was as canny and fraught with suspicion as I'd ever seen. "Darcy's not her usual fare," she said carefully. "He'd not have lasted long."

Unsure of what she meant by that, I asked, "Did he treat her cruelly?"

"No, but he's simple and stupid. Vivienne was already looking at other men."

"Which other men?" I asked, my voice sharpening in defense of my friend.

Her gaze fell. "No one specific. But it was only a matter of time."

Something told me the girl was keeping secrets for the dead, and I could only get from her the information she was willing to part with.

"Tell me, Claudia," I began, turning toward Vivienne's maid, whose eyes were still fixed upon the scheduling diary with a fervent intensity. "Were you aware of any rendezvous between your mistress and the prince?"

"Of course not," she replied, her voice shaking slightly. "I knew nothing about nothing. But it doesn't surprise me; Vivienne always had secrets."

"Secrets can be dangerous, especially in the hands of someone like her," I mused, watching as Claudia clutched the diary to her chest with a vehemence that made me uneasy. "It could be her secrets that got her killed, which is why I would like to know about your mistress. Not to judge her, but to find her killer."

"If I knew, I would tell. I swear it! Vivienne was more than just my mistress," she whispered, her eyes suddenly brimming with tears. "She was my idol, my everything. I would have done anything for her—anything."

"Even if it meant putting yourself in danger?" I asked gently, sensing that there was more to Claudia's obsession with Vivienne than mere admiration.

"Especially then," she insisted, her voice cracking under the weight of her emotions. "I would have willingly given my life for hers."

"Oh, Claudia," I said, my heart aching for the grief-stricken woman before me. "I'm going to tell you something I learned recently."

She sniffed, looking up at me with young eyes shining with pain.

"True love is not blind devotion; it is seeing someone for who they truly are, flaws and all, and loving them despite—or perhaps because of—those imperfections. Vivienne was a complicated woman, and I didn't know her well, but I know she didn't treat you kindly all of the time. And I hope that you will expect your next employer to treat you with a little more humanity."

"I will...Miss Mahoney," Claudia said after a moment, meeting my gaze with a mixture of gratitude and pain. "You have given me much to think about."

"Might I borrow this?" I closed the diary, aching to pore over the last two years of Vivienne's life. "I'll return it as soon as I'm able."

She looked as if she might decline, but then shook herself and fisted her hands in her lap. "If you use it only to continue your investigation into Vivienne's death."

"For no other purpose. I'll care for it better than the family Bible," I assured her, my resolve strengthened by her plea. "I cannot promise that what I find will bring you peace, but I can't see Darcy hanged for a murder he didn't commit, and I'm just as dedicated as you are to finding the killer."

"Thank you," she whispered. "That is all I ask."

❦

MY MIND RACED as I hired a hackney, poring over the pages once ensconced within.

How did the threads of Albert Victor and the Mediterranean island entwine with the tragic fate of Vivienne Bloomfield-Smythe? Were these simply the frivolous distractions of the elite, or did they bear the stain of darker deeds?

Once home, I locked myself away from the world, looking over every scrap of knowledge that had come into my possession. The diary lay open before me, its secrets sprawled across the desk like a splayed corpse awaiting autopsy. Each entry was a clue, each appointment a potential motive or alibi. But the puzzle was maddeningly incomplete, the edges jagged and ill-fitting.

"Damnation," I breathed, pressing my fingertips to my temples as if I could physically squeeze the answers from my beleaguered brain. My heart galloped a frantic rhythm, echoing through the hollow expanse of my chest. This was more than just a search for truth; it was a quest to quiet the restless spirits that haunted my sleepless nights—Mary Kelly's among them.

One thing was clear—to get to the bottom of this mystery, I needed to assemble some of the players. It was risky, but it was my best chance at unraveling the knotted threads and exposing the truth. Their voices, their memories, their guilt and innocence—I needed them arrayed before me as palpably as the pieces on a chessboard. I needed to see how they moved. How they reacted.

What I needed was Grayson Croft. The one man of my acquaintance who navigated the murky waters of law and disorder with an unyielding sense of justice, his moral compass steady even in the face of tempests.

I would need to appeal to him, to convince him of the necessity of this unconventional ploy. For the mystery of Vivienne's murder was not merely a knot to be untangled, but a labyrinth within which we might easily lose ourselves. Only together could Croft and I hope to trace the labyrinth's path, to follow it to its heart, where the truth lurked, veiled in shadows.

Chapter Eleven

B ut first, I had to get permission.

The moment I stepped into the dimly lit Shiloh room of the Velvet Glove, a shiver of foreboding slithered down my spine. The air felt dense and heavy around the two towering figures locked in a silent tableau of fury.

Jorah and Night Horse stood like titans on the precipice of war, their postures rigid, fists clenched as if they were seconds away from letting their tempers explode into violence. The shadows cast by the flickering gas lamps danced upon their hardened faces, highlighting the stark lines of tension that had drawn their brows together and pinched their lips into thin, unforgiving lines.

"Good evening, gentlemen," I said, my voice laced with feigned nonchalance. Their stances, rigid as iron bars, spoke of a quarrel interrupted. The air crackled with their unsaid words a silent war waged with glares that could flay flesh.

At my voice, Jorah shifted his piercing eyes to me, the tempest within them momentarily abated. Like a disciplined soldier, he regained his composure with an effort that was almost visible, his steely gaze betraying nothing of what words had passed between him and his right-hand man.

"Miss Mahoney," he greeted me, his faint Eastern accent wrapping around my name like a caress, albeit one that couldn't mask the undercurrent of rage in his tone.

"Fiona," Night Horse muttered by way of greeting, his voice rough as gravel. A muscle twitched in his jaw, betraying the restraint it took to hold his tongue.

My desire to probe further was abruptly curtailed as the door creaked open once more, admitting two figures who couldn't have been at starker odds with each other. George Tunstall, Darcy O'Dowd's manager, entered first; his sour countenance seemed etched from stone, his lips set in a permanent sneer of distaste. He moved with the air of a man perpetually dissatisfied with his lot, as though life itself had dealt him a losing hand he could neither fold nor accept.

Behind him, a shadow of the formidable prizefighter I knew loomed into the room. Darcy's broad shoulders were hunched, the usual fire in his eyes now extinguished, replaced by a hollow pain that spoke of sleepless nights and a heart weighed down by grief and dread.

"Evenin', Fiona," he murmured, his voice a hoarse whisper of its former booming cheer. His haunted eyes met mine, and in them, I read the turmoil of a soul torn asunder by Vivienne Bloomfield-Smythe's untimely demise and the gallows that beckoned with grim promise.

"Darcy," I acknowledged him quietly, my own heart clenching at the sight of him so diminished, so lost without the woman he had loved.

"Still parading about with this lot, then?" he teased halfheartedly.

"Good friends are hard to come by," I retorted, my tone devoid of humor.

"Miss Mahoney," Tunstall said with a curt nod, the lines on his face etched deeper by scorn. He despised this room, the company, the entire sordid affair, yet here he remained. Like all of us, bound by threads of necessity, woven into a tapestry of deceit.

"Let's not stand on ceremony," I said, stepping further into the room. "We've graver matters to attend to than whatever has your hackles raised." I let my gaze linger on Jorah and Night Horse a moment longer, daring them to contradict me.

Night Horse shot Jorah a final warning look, a silent promise of unfinished business, before turning his attention toward me, an unspoken truce forged in the face of shared adversity.

I withdrew the handkerchief from within the confines of my cloak, unfolding the delicate fabric with a carefulness that belied the unrest simmering in my blood. "Does this belong to any of you?" I asked, voice steady as I held it out for inspection.

Jorah gazed at the handkerchief with an inscrutable expression before he tersely shook his head. Night Horse followed suit, eyes cold and unreadable, while Tunstall merely scoffed at the notion.

"Never seen it," Darcy murmured.

"The police will be keen to have evidence such as this," I said, tucking the fabric back into my sleeve. "Croft could follow this to the real murderer, leading the investigation away from you, Darcy." The words hung like a guillotine above our heads, and we were all too aware of how the blade could fall in any direction.

A spark of hope lit Darcy's eyes. "What's that stitched on it, then?"

"C.F.—Clarissa Fairchild's initials," I continued, watching their reactions closely. "It could imply the baroness's guilt, or perhaps she is being framed."

"Or perhaps it's a lover's token, discarded after a tryst," Jorah suggested, his voice steady but his eyes betraying a flicker of concern.

"Or it was dropped before the murder occurred and has nothing to do with Vivienne's murder," Tunstall pointed out.

"Regardless," I pressed on, "I need to know what to tell Croft—and what not to. He has the resources to investigate its origins properly." I leaned forward, lowering my voice. "But I don't wish to reveal anything that might...compromise present company."

"Share what you must, Fiona," Jorah finally said, his words carefully measured. "I trust you'll know what will keep our necks from stretching."

Night Horse nodded his agreement.

Darcy's hands clenched into fists, the knuckles whitening. "The truth won't bring her back," he murmured, a pained edge cutting through his grief. "But it must be found, so justice can be done."

I perched on the edge of an opulent chaise, idly tracing the embroidery of the handkerchief with my fingers as I observed the men before me. Darcy's silhouette was hunched, the broad shoulders that once seemed capable of bearing the world now bowed under an invisible weight.

"Then it is decided," I said quietly.

Their assent granted me a measure of relief, but also a shroud of apprehension. As I turned to leave, the tension between Jorah and Night Horse still crackled in the background, a storm on the horizon that promised no safe harbor.

"There's something else." I paused, unsure of how to proceed.

"Out with it," Darcy urged.

"This flower stitched into the handkerchief," I began, my voice laced with a gentle firmness meant to soothe Darcy's troubled spirit. "It seems this symbol might be more significant than we initially believed."

His eyes flickered with a spark of curiosity, but it was quickly doused by his prevailing sorrow. "And what does that have to do with Vivienne?" he asked, his brogue thickened by grief.

"Vivienne's past is a tapestry woven with many threads," I replied. "The green carnation is often a token amongst those harboring forbidden affections for someone of their own sex. This flower depicted beneath the initials is a carnation, I've come to realize. So perhaps there is a sapphic connection. I mean, consider Claudia's obsession with her—"

"Which is enough to make her a strong suspect," Tunstall cut in, his tone harsh, like the strike of a match.

"Certainly," I replied, "and consider this: Vivienne is known to have made a bid for the baron and lost to Lady Clarissa Fairchild. Yet we should not dismiss the possibility that her connection is actually with the *baroness* and ventured into...intimate territories."

"Exploring sapphic love with the green carnation as their emblem?" Jorah's voice was pensive. "That's a bold theory."

"Except," Night Horse interjected, his gaze sharp enough to slice through the foggy shadows of the Velvet Glove, "the flower stitched here is white, not green."

"An oversight or a deliberate choice?" I mused aloud, though my question hung unanswered between us.

Tunstall scoffed, his voice gruff with disdain. "Such fancies are best left to playwrights and detective novels,

Miss Mahoney. Vivienne was never one to indulge in floral metaphors of any kind."

"Nor did she seem one to trifle with baronesses," Darcy added, his tone edged with a bitterness that spoke of more than just the loss of a lover. It bore the acrid taste of betrayal.

"Could be nothing," I allowed, unwilling to spar with him when there were larger games afoot. "But that's why I think Croft is the one with the most ability to follow this clue to its origin."

Jorah and Night Horse were glaring at each other like two storm clouds ready to clash. The air bristled with their silent confrontation dark looks exchanged with the subtlety of a loaded pistol beneath a dinner jacket.

"Your dispute seems a private affair," I ventured, attempting to gauge the crux of their tension.

"Private affairs have a way of becoming public display," Night Horse retorted, his voice low and dangerous.

"Especially when blood has been spilled," Jorah added, fixing Night Horse with a glare that could freeze the Thames over.

"Enough," I said sharply, rising to stand. "We are allies in *this*, whether by choice or circumstance. Let's not forget that."

The room settled into a begrudging truce as I folded the handkerchief, tucking it away like a card yet to be played. The scent of old leather and lingering tobacco wrapped around us—a shroud for secrets too perilous to unearth.

"Then we're agreed," I concluded. "The handkerchief will go to Croft, along with our collective silence on certain matters."

A chorus of reluctant nods followed, each man steeped in his own brew of suspicion and fear.

"I was half hoping the evidence would point to Drumft," I muttered.

"Drumft," Jorah growled, the name leaving his lips like a curse. "He never treated Vivienne as she deserved. Used her beauty for his gain and discarded her spirit like waste." The scorn in his voice was palpable, laced with a venom that suggested a personal vendetta against the Prussian dignitary.

"More than that," Darcy chimed in, "she told me of his beatings. Oswald's temper is infamous, but with Vivienne... It was a cruelty that ran deeper."

"Why do you think he hurt her?" I asked, a cold fury rising inside me. "Is he a sadist, you think?"

Jorah's expression tightened, the lines around his eyes deepening. He hesitated, then released a breath he seemed to have been holding for an eternity. "He's an antisemite."

"What?" I gasped, when no one else made a sound.

"Vivienne was more than what the world saw," he confessed, his voice suddenly low and intimate. "The name she bore when we met...was Blumfeld."

"Blumfeld?" Tunstall repeated incredulously, while

Night Horse simply stared, a carefully blank expression advertising that he was ignorant to the revelation.

"She was a Jew," I murmured.

Jorah nodded gravely. "Concealed behind a gentile mask. We were both refugees in the Jewish Quarter when the world was harsher, colder. She shed her heritage like a second skin, lost her accent, and wove a new identity from sheer will. Vivienne used every ounce of her guile and ambition to ascend London's social ladder. She was a fierce soul, even then, determined to escape the squalor and make something of herself."

"Which she did," I said, unable to keep the admiration from my voice. "At great cost." Vivienne's past held more shadows than I had imagined, each one a potential motive wrapped in the fabric of her untimely demise.

"She was remarkable," Darcy agreed, though his tone bore the weight of a man mourning the loss of an era. "But now she's gone, and all that's left are the secrets she kept and the enemies she made."

"Enemies who might kill because of her heritage," I added, the severity of our situation settling over me like a shroud. There was much at stake—more than mere reputations. It was a matter of life and death, tangled in the web of Vivienne's mysterious past.

"Vivienne Bloomfield-Smythe," I mused, the name now holding the power of a once-concealed truth. "A rose by any other name..."

"Can still harbor thorns," Tunstall finished.

"Vivienne had a fire in her," Jorah murmured, the Russian lilt of his accent more pronounced in the somber quiet. "A spirit that even the darkest alleys of Whitechapel couldn't snuff out. And now..." He trailed off, clenching his jaw so tightly that I thought it might shatter.

The hush that fell over the Shiloh room was as thick as the London fog outside, cut only by the occasional crackle from the hearth. Jorah stood apart, his gaze lost in the roaring fire, a man adrift on a sea of regret. His voice, when he finally spoke, carried the weight of a thousand sorrows, each word etched with a pain that seemed to transcend mere grief.

I watched Darcy, the Dublin Destroyer, a man whose reputation for ferocity in the ring was matched only by the depth of his loyalty. He stood silent, the usual spark in his green eyes snuffed out by grief. Yet even in mourning, it was Jorah's anguish that drew my eye—raw and unguarded. I noted this discrepancy, the incongruity of emotion between former lover and current. The observation left me unsettled, a piece of a puzzle I was reluctant to place, for fear it would reveal a picture too grim to face.

It was Darcy who broke the stillness, his voice hollow with shock. "A Jewess," he breathed, his broad shoulders sagging under the weight of this new knowledge. "I wish she'd trusted me enough to tell me...after I trusted her with..."

"It wouldn't have mattered to anyone here," Tunstall

interjected, his usual brusque demeanor faltering. His face, often stern and unreadable, now betrayed a clear sense of astonishment. "How did she manage to keep such a thing secret in a city that thrives on gossip?"

"By being smarter than the lot of us," Jorah answered, a bitter edge to his tone. "And by understanding that some secrets are a matter of survival."

The revelation seemed to settle upon Darcy and Tunstall like ash from an extinguished flame, a stark reminder of the precarious nature of existence in our shadowed corners of society. Disbelief etched itself into every line of their faces, a testament to the woman who'd walked among us, her true identity veiled behind a carefully constructed façade.

"Survival," I echoed softly, the word tasting like iron on my tongue.

The room, cloaked in shadows and the smoke from Jorah's pipe, seemed to shrink under the weight of our collective resolve. I found myself standing, my spine a rigid line against the oppressive silence that had fallen over the Velvet Glove's Shiloh room.

Yet even as the agreement passed our lips, the air remained thick with disquiet. A glance between Jorah and Night Horse spoke volumes of discord—their stances rigid, the space between them charged with silent animosity. I knew not the root of their quarrel, but its presence was like a serpent, coiled and ready to strike at any moment.

Tunstall shook his head, still grappling with the

revelation. "All this time, right under our noses." He looked to Jorah, then to me, a dawning comprehension in his gaze. "There's more to this, isn't there? More you're not saying."

"Perhaps," I allowed, but offered nothing further. In the dance of truth and lies, it was wise to keep one's cards close to one's chest—even amongst allies.

"More will be revealed in time," Jorah stated, a cryptic note coloring his baritone. "For now, we must tread carefully, Fiona. There are eyes upon us, hungry for the slightest misstep."

"Agreed," I conceded, feeling the weight of those unseen eyes upon my back. In my nightmares, those eyes belonged to the Ripper.

I bade them goodnight and left the Shiloh room, happy to be rid of an excess of brooding, tense, and emotionally stunted masculine company.

The cobbles were slick beneath my boots, a treacherous sheen of recent rain reflecting the gray skies like a dull mirror. The Velvet Glove's heavy door closed behind me with a muffled thud, as if sealing away the fragile alliance we'd just brokered. London wrapped around me, a cloak woven from shadows and secrets, its chill seeping into my bones.

I exhaled a breath I hadn't realized I was holding, watching it form a spectral wisp in the air before vanishing into oblivion. My footsteps were soft whispers against stone as I hastened down the alley, yet something pricked at the nape of my neck—a sensation that

I was not alone, an instinct honed by years navigating the underbelly of this city.

A footfall echoed mine, a half-beat out of sync. I quickened my pace, heart pounding a staccato rhythm that thrummed in my ears. Another step, heavier, more deliberate, shattered the silence behind me. My blood turned to ice. Fear's icy tendrils clutched at my throat, throttling the scream that dared to escape.

I glanced back to find a hulking shadow at the entrance to the alley.

Panic lent wings to my feet as I broke into a run. The alley stretched before me, an endless void swallowing my hopes of sanctuary. I could hear the ragged breath of my pursuer, feel the proximity of danger breathing down my neck. Was it the killer who had silenced Vivienne so brutally? A shiver cascaded down my spine at the thought.

Right before I would have burst onto the safety of the Strand, a strong arm locked around me like an iron band, cutting off my ability to scream for help.

Chapter Twelve

"Fi-Fiona, it's me." The voice, when it finally cut through the murk, was a balm to the frisson of dread skittering along my spine. Recognition dawned, though not without its own brand of disquiet.

"Darcy Brendan O'Dowd, I should box your ears in for startling me so!" I put a palm over my still-racing heart.

He stood before me, his familiar form somehow misplaced within the slim alleyway. "Sorry, Fi... I didn't mean to scare you." His face, cast half in shadow, bore lines of worry and something else—an unspoken burden that weighed heavily.

"It's all right. I'd already worked myself into a lather."

Why had I seen an enemy before I recognized a friend? I pondered this silently, even as relief shuddered through me. Alleys were the haunts of death, where women disappeared into the night, never to return, save for in horrified whispers and loud headlines. Where Jack the Ripper did his work, all except for the room in which he'd killed Mary.

For that room had allowed him to take his time.

"What's wrong, Darcy?" I asked, sensing something was urgent. "Why follow me into the dark?"

He shifted, a gladiator uncertain of his arena. "I have a confession to make, Fi. But if it goes further than this alley, it could mean ruin for us both. Do you understand? It could mean the end of everything." Those words, ominous and fraught with potential malevolence, stole the warmth from my blood.

"Why tell me at all, then?" I asked through the trepidation still knotting my guts.

His fingers dug into my arms as he gripped them, eyes wilder than I'd ever seen them. "We need your help, Fiona."

"Help?" I echoed. Trust was a currency in short supply these days, and even Darcy's earnest gaze could not purchase it outright. "We? Who are you talking about?"

His eyes searched mine, beseeching me for understanding, and I knew that whatever secrets lay buried within his heart, they must be akin to the shards of glass littering the grimy alley underfoot—sharp enough to wound deeply. "Aye, help. There's more at play here than you know. More than anyone knows."

"Calm down," I replied, my voice steadier than I felt. "Speak your piece, Darcy—anything you say will be safe with me."

His fingers twitched, and he exhaled a breath that had been held captive by some unspeakable burden. The dim light from the street flickered, casting his features into stark relief, revealing the torment etched into the lines of his once-familiar face.

"Fi," he began, voice barely a whisper, "there's something about me that you don't know. Somethin' that I've kept tucked away beneath my skin like a tattoo I can't let anyone else see."

I frowned, the taut thread of apprehension within me winding tighter, ready to snap. "You're speaking in riddles, Darcy. Be plain. Tell me true."

He hesitated, the muscle in his jaw working furiously before he turned his wrist to show me the little symbol inked over his pulse point. "I'm a member of the Order of the Green Carnation," he said at last. "Georgie isn't just my manager. He's my..." He did his best to find a word that could encompass all he felt.

"He's your...lover?" I supplied.

His eyes glimmered with moisture. "He's my everything."

My mind reeled as I grappled with the gravity of his confession. The order was whispered about in hushed tones, a fraternity of men bound together by their shared, forbidden desires. To be one of them was to court scandal and disgrace at best, and possible time in prison.

"Sweet Christ..." My voice trailed off, lost amidst the swirling fog of shock that enveloped me. A man's predilections were his own affair, but the revelation of Darcy's allegiance to such a clandestine order opened up so many more variables for investigation. Avenues he was right to fear.

"Is it so hard to believe?" His eyes, usually so full of fight, now pleaded for understanding.

"No, not hard to believe," I replied, my heart aching with empathy. "But it's dangerous to admit, even to me."

"True, but there's more. It involves someone dear to both our hearts." He paused, swallowing hard, desperate gaze boring into mine. "Flynn."

"Flynn?" I echoed, the name of my lost brother sounding like a sacred incantation on his lips.

"Your brother, God rest him, he was...he was...he was the love of my fecking life, Fiona. My heart *belonged* to him," Darcy confessed, each word heavy with the weight of unshed tears. "Some of it still does. So much that seeing what parts of him also live in you makes me weep for wanting. But Fiona...he gave me his for safe-keeping as well. And I kept it until they killed him."

A silent sob clawed at my throat, caught between the sharp edges of bereavement and an inexplicable sense of happiness. Flynn, who had always been a beacon of strength and laughter in a grim world, had known love—a fierce, secret love—in the midst of all the darkness. It pained me that such tenderness had been cloaked in shadow, never to see the light of our cruel society.

That Darcy had to grieve his loss alone.

"Flynn?" I murmured again, the name now a lament. "Oh, Darcy. Why didn't you say before?"

"Do you think your father would have understood? Would Finn? Or Nola?" he asked, his voice breaking. "We *had* to hide, to pretend. But in those stolen moments, we were free. He made me feel invincible."

"Invincible," I repeated, the word bittersweet on my tongue. I knew what it was to hold such a love, only to have it snatched away by the cold hand of death.

The alley felt suddenly oppressive, the shadows around us teeming with ghosts of secrets and lost chances. I reached out tentatively, placing my hand upon his arm. "You had to mourn him alone," I said around hot tears leaking from my eyes. "I'm so sorry, Darcy."

His gaze met mine, and in it, I saw a reflection of my own sorrow, a shared understanding that transcended words.

"Whatever comes, I stand with you," I vowed, the conviction in my voice chasing away the last remnants of doubt.

Flynn had loved him. That alone was testament enough to the content of Darcy's character.

"Thank you," he whispered, gratitude and resolve mingling in his expression. We were two souls, bound by grief and a yearning for justice. Together, we would face whatever darkness lay ahead.

"What do you say to a drink?" I asked, the damp chill of the alley clinging to my bones. It was a tomb of whispers and shadows, each one heavy with the ghosts of our past. It was no place for the living.

WE SETTLED into the dimly lit corner of an old pub, far from prying eyes. The hushed murmur of other patrons became a distant hum as we leaned into the intimacy of our shared grief.

"Fi, I need you to understand why I've come to you in such desperate times," Darcy began, his eyes darting away before returning to mine with a tumultuous resolve.

"Speak your heart," I said softly, but my own heart drummed against my ribs with trepidation.

"Your family... They were heroes to me," he confessed, "and the night they were taken, a part of me died with them."

I closed my eyes, summoning the courage to revisit that harrowing night. "Father led them out, filled with righteous fire to aid a family terrorized by those British tyrants. They left Fayne, so young and eager at eleven, in my care."

"God, Fi..." Darcy's voice cracked, and his hand

reached across the table to find mine. "I didn't know that."

"Little Fayne could not be caged by fear or duty," I continued, tightening my grip on his hand. "I put us to bed, and he slipped out like a wisp of smoke in the dark."

"He initially stayed behind?" His question was barely audible, laden with dread.

He knew how the story ended.

"Only when the echoes of gunfire and explosions startled me from slumber." My voice quivered as I opened my eyes to meet his stormy gaze. "By the time I found my way onto the street, it was too late. Their bodies...displayed like grotesque banners of defeat... even little Fayne."

A tear dripped into Darcy's ale, mirroring my own silent anguish. The loss of Flynn had carved a hollow space within us both, a void where once there had been joy and laughter. But I had six more deaths to mourn. My father Frank Mahoney. And my lovely brothers.

"Fi, I swear on their beloved memory, I had nothing to do with Vivienne's murder," he said fervently. "Upon my love for Flynn, I'd never harm another soul in such a way. Neither Georgie nor I could have anything to do with it." His eyes burned with sincerity, yet the seeds of suspicion, once sown, were not easily uprooted.

"I believe you," I said honestly, though my mind was a maelstrom of unease. "But I'm not convinced of anyone else's innocence at the moment, not even Mr. Tunstall's."

"Georgie is many things, driven by ambition and blinded by jealousy at times," Darcy conceded, "but we are bound by more than just shared secrets, Fi. Our hearts, though hidden, beat with the same rhythm."

"Did Vivienne know of your affair with Mr. Tunstall?" I queried.

"From the very beginning." His lip wobbled, and I could see in him the boy I once knew. "The farce of our entanglement was her idea," he revealed. "In public, she and I were a perfect couple that shared a genuine affection. In private, we were both free to be ourselves."

"Was Vivienne...?" I wasn't certain of the word I needed, but he caught my meaning.

"Nah. She liked her men. I'm thinking a bird or two had been thrown in the mix for sport, but in all, she chased the blokes. Or, rather, they chased her." The specter of a smile haunted his lips as he remembered Vivienne fondly before grief stole the expression and turned it back to stone. "We have to find who did this to her. We have to make them pay."

"Whatever it takes," I promised. "Is that possible to explore the Order of the Green Carnation without exposing those involved to ruin?"

"I don't know." Darcy shook his head before letting it slump low over his shoulders. "But if it means justice for Viv, then...I can't be a coward and hide from who I am anymore."

I shaped my palm to his cheek, thumbing away the next tear from bristled skin. "You are not a coward to protect your love from those who would profane it, Darcy. I will do all I can to protect you..."

My words evoked more tears rather than the opposite, as intended. Darcy took my hand in his rough palm and placed a deferential kiss on my knuckles. "For Flynn," he whispered.

"For anyone who had to keep a such love a secret out of fear."

Chapter Thirteen

"Detective Croft's office is just here," the constable guiding me offered with the kind of deference I wasn't accustomed to receiving from law enforcement. His uniform gleamed with the sheen of newness, worn by someone who had yet to truly experience the darker side of London's underbelly.

I traced him through the labyrinthine corridors of Scotland Yard, my boots thudding against the cold stone floor with a steady rhythm that matched the pounding pulse at my throat. The walls were lined with dark wood paneling and dimly lit by flickering gas lamps, casting long shadows that danced along the floor. The scent of dampness mingled with the acrid aroma of stale tobacco smoke, giving the place a palpable sense of decay.

Of course I knew where Croft's office was, but I

allowed him to be helpful. The lamps cast anemic pools of light onto walls lined with somber portraits of stern-faced men who seemed to scrutinize my passage with silent reproach.

The round-faced constable rapped sharply on a heavy wooden door, its surface marred by years of use, and announced my presence before stepping aside.

"Thank you." I offered him my most solicitous smile, betraying none of the trepidation that clenched tightly around my heart.

A brass nameplate read, DET. INSPECTOR A. GRAYSON CROFT.

A? I'd not noted that before. How had I known Croft all this time and not known that Grayson wasn't, in fact, his Christian name?

The door creaked open, and I stepped into a realm that bore the soul of a man I was acquainted with, but apparently knew not at all.

Detective A. Grayson Croft's sanctum was a chaotic symphony of paper and ink: case files sprawled across his desk, spilling onto the leather-bound tomes that lined the shelves like soldiers at attention. A single window, smeared with the grime of London's relentless industry, allowed a weak shaft of daylight to penetrate the gloom, casting angular shadows across his brutal features.

"Miss Mahoney," Croft greeted me without lifting his gaze from the documents splayed before him. "To what do I owe the pleasure?"

"Detective," I replied, crossing the threshold fully and ignoring the droll sarcasm in his tone. "Information has come to light in the Vivienne Bloomfield-Smythe case," I began, withdrawing the handkerchief and a sheaf of notes I had meticulously compiled. "I learned something about this handkerchief that could very well be the key."

Croft's eyes, sharp as an eagle's and just as predatory, lifted to meet mine. In that moment, the connection between us was palpable—a tenuous bond forged of a mutual desire for justice.

He curled his fingers around the handkerchief, plucking it from my hand with a gentleness that belied his gruff exterior. He studied the embroidered cloth, furrowing his brow as if trying to decipher a hidden message within its folds.

"I was half ready to chase you down and toss your house to retrieve this evidence, but I knew that it was safe in your clutches and would find its way back to me with a new story." He leveled a flinty gaze at me. "If this is another finger pointed at the royal family, it'd better be a smoking gun, Fiona. I'm already in deep water for asking the first round of questions, which cleared His Highness, Albert Victor, from all suspicion."

"It did?" I squeaked, not having heard anything of the sort. "What happened?"

"That, I am forbidden to speak of," he groused. "Now, tell me what this scrap of lace means. Knowing you, there's a litany of theories accompanying this," he prompted, his voice a low rumble that reverberated through the close atmosphere of the room.

"A litany?" I huffed. "Hardly that, though now I'm disinclined to share any of my hard-won findings with you."

"You may as well speak your mind, Miss Mahoney," Croft urged, his heavy sigh tinged with impatience. "Time is of the essence." He turned the handkerchief over in his hands, the fabric whispering secrets against his fingertips.

"Detective inspector, I have reason to suspect that there may have been...personal entanglements beyond mere enmity between the baroness, Clarissa Fairchild, and Vivienne."

"Personal?" His brow arched, the question unspoken but hanging like fog in the room. "We've found no evidence to suggest anything beyond a romantic rivalry that was decided two decades ago."

"But what if the romantic rivalry had nothing to do with the baron?" I asked, my voice a hushed confession amidst the rigid spines of case files that lined the shelves, witnesses to countless unsolved mysteries. "What if it was between the baroness and Vivienne all along? Certainly such an affair is worth killing for."

"The baroness and Vivienne," Croft mused, placing the handkerchief on his desk as if it were a fallen petal rather than potential evidence. "Do you have more than hearsay to back up your theory?"

"You already know I found this handkerchief by the

boot of the knight's kit," I said. "C.F. could very easily be Clarissa Fairchild. And then there's this flower stitched below. Are you familiar with Order of the Green Carnation?"

"Can't say that I am," he replied.

"It's a clandestine club where people who are romantically interested in their own sex can find companionship. They often use it on lapel pins, tattoos, bookmarks, and other such personal items, like this handkerchief, to find people of similar tastes."

"As a theory, it's a bit far-fetched. The blossom on this handkerchief isn't green." Croft's scowl deepened. "Besides, I do not concern myself with people's private inclinations, Miss Mahoney, unless they cause harm to others."

"Your integrity is commendable, detective," I admitted, respect threading through my tone like silver through the darkness.

"Integrity has little currency if it does not champion the cause of justice." He leaned back in his chair, the creak of leather punctuating his resolve.

"I thought perhaps this depiction of a carnation on the handkerchief might be pointing in that direction," I challenged. "That and what Dr. Phillips said about the slight build of the killer made me wonder if Vivienne's murderer could be a woman with less-than-platonic feelings for her. I know Claudia is more bereft than is seemly for anyone to be after the loss of an employer...

Surely as a detective you're aware of how love and madness walk hand in hand."

At that, he paused, his eyes tracking a thought around the room. "Why not bring this to me sooner?" he asked. "A few days have passed since you'd access to the scene to clean it."

His keen awareness caught my hesitation. "I didn't know if I could trust you with the whole truth."

He lifted a brow. "There's more?"

I knotted my fingers together, the words threatening to strangle me before they were spoken. "I'm only telling you this because I think it will ultimately help to clear Darcy's name."

His visage darkened. "Go on."

I felt like I was chewing on ashes, but I went on. "I discovered that Darcy and Tunstall were—are—lovers," I whispered, my voice barely audible even to my own ears. "I cannot help but wonder if this might have provided Mr. Tunstall with a stronger motive to harm Vivienne."

As much as I didn't want Darcy to lose another love, I didn't want him to hang.

"Miss Mahoney," Croft said, his voice grave. "You must understand that divulging such information can have serious consequences for all involved."

"I know," I admitted, guilt clawing at my heart as I recalled Aidan, my late fiancé, and the terrible secrets he had kept hidden from me. Love could blind even the most perceptive of souls, and I was no exception. "But if we are to find Vivienne's killer, we must consider every possibility, no matter how painful."

Croft's fingers ceased their dance over the scattered case files as he regarded me with an inscrutable gaze, his eyes carrying the emerald of my isle muted by the stormy hues of London's own tumultuous skies. "Miss Mahoney," he began, his voice resonant within the confines of his office, a sanctuary of law and order amidst the chaos that had overtaken the city's streets, "I don't give two ripe shits what Darcy and Tunstall are up to in their own time. My only duty here is to unearth the truth behind Vivienne's murder."

"Thank you," I whispered, the relief coursing through me tangling with a knotted sense of trepidation. I hoped the information would help rather than hinder the investigation. And, though I couldn't say this to Darcy, I wasn't convinced as he about Tunstall's innocence.

"I'll see you out, Miss Mahoney. I'm at the end of my shift."

We rose from our seats, and as we made our way out of his office, the din of Scotland Yard enveloped us—the murmur of constables discussing leads, the clatter of typewriters documenting the deeds of the day. Croft guided me back through the maze of corridors, his presence a bulwark against the pervasive darkness hovering around Vivienne's death.

"Why don't you stop 'round for tea?" he suggested, shocking me. "Amelia has been asking after you."

As fond as I remained of Amelia Croft, I couldn't bring myself to look his older sister in eye right now—the weight of their secret pressed too heavily against my beleaguered conscience at the moment.

I stepped into the night through the door Croft held open for me and was pleased when he took his pipe and tobacco from his pocket. The scent was among my favorite things in the world, though I'd die before admitting it to him.

Croft stared up at the clouds as if he might spy a star through their ranks. "I thought Darcy might have his cap set for your affections, so warm was the air between the both of you."

I caught his side-eyed glare as I glanced over at him, and hid a smile. Croft was many things, but subtle wasn't one of them.

"It was my brother, Flynn, who caught his eye, and heart, years ago," I explained, the new information still settling a new layer over my memories. "I can't help but wish Flynn and he..." My throat closed over a choked emotion, and I had to clear it twice in order to speak. "Had my brothers survived, they might have had a life together, which means Vivienne might have lived, as well."

"You learn not to do that when you're a detective," Grayson said, his hand hovering over my shoulder without landing before he returned it to his side. "Take care not to focus on the *if only*. That way, madness lies."

"You're right," I conceded, falling into step with him

as we walked in the vague direction of the train he'd take home to Lambeth. "I shouldn't wish against death. He always wins."

"Loss, I've discovered... It carves into us, hollows us out," he confided, a rare glimpse of vulnerability surfacing in his eyes. "I believe that it is our ability to endure such hardships that ultimately defines who we are. And you are more resilient than most, I've noticed."

"Thank you." My thoughts drifted to the countless nights I had spent poring over old letters and photographs, seeking some semblance of comfort in the remnants of a life that had been so cruelly snatched away from Mary. From me. "Sometimes, I cannot help but feel that the past is a specter that haunts my every step. Like a needy ghost that refuses to let me be."

"I'm not immune to that feeling," Croft said, a faint smile curving his lips as he regarded me intently. "It is not the past that holds me captive so much as it is the unknown. To find peace, I know I have to find the truth first, even if the truth is more painful than the kindness of ignorance." His voice was a low thrum filled with a resonance that spoke of kindred spirits forged in the crucible of pain.

The intimacy of our exchange lingered between us like the final notes of a requiem as we strolled through the muted daylight. The cobblestones were slick with the remnants of a morning drizzle. The thrumming pulse of London life swirled around us—a stark contrast to the somber cadence of our footsteps. The leaden sky hung oppressively low, mirroring the weight that pressed upon my chest.

"Detective Croft," I began, my voice scarcely above a whisper, yet slicing through the cacophony of the city's heart like the sharpest of blades. "What if... What if I knew a truth that would cause you and your sister pain, but would answer a question you've been chasing for years?"

He halted mid-stride, his countenance etched with lines of wary anticipation. His eyes, those twin pools of fathomless inquiry, fixed upon me with an intensity that beckoned the truth forth from its shadowy recess.

"There is no such truth...except..." His eyes widened, features hardening into stone.

"Your nephew," I whispered. "The baby Amelia gave up in her youth."

He backed up one step. Then another, forcing a few pedestrians to change gait and walk around him. He remained solely focused on me, verdant eyes alight with a fire I'd never witnessed. A dark flame. One that could never be extinguished.

"You gave the child to Katherine Riley," I continued, the words tumbling out in a headlong rush. "The woman who worked as an illegal adoption agency for... desperate mothers."

"Desperate" usually meaning the unwed or prostitutes.

A silence fell between us, heavy and suffocating. My heart hammered against my ribcage, each beat a metronome marking the passage into forbidden territories.

"You know I was hired to clean the Katherine Riley murder scene, and it was there I found out what she'd been up to. Katherine was taking her placement fee from the mother and then..." Something about the darkness in his face made it impossible to finish my sentence.

"Then...what?" The question was spoken in a voice so low, I might have imagined the vibrations of it.

I frantically searched my brain for anything that could soften the blow.

"Then *what*, Fiona?"

Every part of me was trembling. My next words would shatter the thin veneer of hope he and Amelia had clung to the many years since she was forced to adopt out a baby she couldn't raise at sixteen.

"I don't know what happened, for certain, but..." I swallowed, or attempted to. "But in the ashes of her fireplace I found...I found...tiny remains."

I expected a storm. A tempestuous reaction as violent as the pain I could read in his eyes as the full implications of my revelation sank in.

What met me was a cold so arctic, it hurt my lungs to breathe in his vicinity.

"You. *Knew?*" The word was laced with incredulity and the sharp tang of betrayal.

"Grayson, please understand," I implored, my hands

reaching out only to fall limply by my sides when he flinched away.

"You sat at my table. Befriended my sister. Listened as she spoke of her little boy out there somewhere, and the whole time you—" He broke off, turning away and stalking through the few pedestrians blinking at us both in surprise.

Paying them no heed, I followed him, taking two trotting steps to every furious one of his.

"It was not my secret to share," I explained. "I—I wanted to protect you. To save Amelia from—"

"Protect?" he echoed, the fury in his voice rising like a tempest. "You've *no right* to decide what pain to spare us. What truth to hide!"

"I know. You're right. Grayson, I..." Words failed me; they retreated into the shadowed corners of my mind, leaving me defenseless before his wrath.

"It'd better be a long time before I see you again, Fiona Mahoney," he said, his wrath a darkness I couldn't comprehend. One I hadn't known he possessed. "And the next time you meddle at one of my crime scenes, I'll throw you in a fucking cell and see you dragged in front of a magistrate."

"I'm sorry, Croft," I whispered, my heart aching with guilt. "I didn't want to hurt you, but I couldn't keep silent any longer."

"I mean it." He spat on the ground next to the hem of my dress, an insult I deserved. "Keep the demon of death that follows you away from me and mine."

He turned on his heel, the tails of his coat flapping like a raven taking flight—as if he could escape the specter of his own pain and loss.

Escape the messenger of death.

Me.

"Grayson!" My plea dissolved into the chill air, unheeded. I watched him stride away, every step driving a nail into the coffin of our nascent trust.

Guilt gnawed at my insides like a famished rodent. He'd said the truth was what he hungered for over ignorance.

Was the truth a poison I had unwittingly administered? Would it eat away at him until he succumbed to its toxins?

A sense of loss enveloped me, creeping through my bones as surely as the evening fog that began to roll off the Thames. I watched his retreating figure become a mere silhouette against the backdrop of London's sprawling indifference.

I stood alone, the cold bite of London's disdainful breeze a stark contrast to the heat of my churning emotions. Croft's bitter departure left me adrift in an ocean of guilt, the briny taste of regret on my lips. His words, a barbed arrow, had found their mark, and I reeled from the impact.

Drawing a shuddering breath, I wrapped my arms around myself, not for warmth but as a futile attempt at self-comfort. The fabric of my coat felt rough against my palms, a tactile reminder of the harsh reality that had just unfolded. My heart grieved, not only for the friendship that now seemed irreparably torn but also for the man who bore the weight of unspeakable loss.

My eyes, stinging with the threat of tears, refused to release them. It was not the time for weakness.

I straightened my shoulders, feeling the invisible mantle of responsibility settle upon them once more. Each step forward felt laborious, like wading through the mire of my own making. But move I must, for the dead could not cry out for themselves.

"Justice," I whispered to the uncaring wind. Vivienne still had none of it. Nor did Mary.

So many women lay in unmarked or unknown graves. In rivers and oceans. In gardens and forests. The violence that ended them hidden from the blind gaze of justice.

"Forgive me," I said once more, though I knew the words were but a whisper in the void. Forgiveness was a luxury I could ill afford. My path was set, and I must follow it to the end—be it redemption or ruin.

With a final glance toward the direction Croft had vanished, I turned away, my heart heavy but my spirit unyielding.

There was work to be done.

Always.

And as was true for so much labor a woman must take upon herself, no one but me seemed inclined to see it through.

Chapter Fourteen

I'd almost missed the fight.

A deceased mother-in-law in Mayfair would pay every bill I owed next month, and I couldn't pass up the job. I'd underestimated the intensity of evening traffic on the Strand during the fight and barely made it in time to watch one of the matches meet its blood-soaked end.

A deafening roar crashed over me as I stepped into the dank underground fighting pit. A cacophony of raucous noise, an operatic din composed of humanity's basest notes. The air thickened with the stench of sweat and ale, mingling into a heady perfume that saturated the underbelly of London's night. Frenetic, violent shadows danced along the walls, flickering like the very flames of Hades, as anticipation gripped my throat in a vise as unyielding as iron shackles.

"Come for the blood sport, pretty bird?" A voice

slithered into my ear, the speaker remaining unseen behind me. "Why don't you sit in me lap?"

I threw my elbow into his flesh and pressed forward, ignoring the taunt and the grasping fingers. My boots stuck slightly to the sawdust-strewn floor, each step a testament to the violence this place had seen. My heart thrummed an erratic beat, mirroring the palpable excitement that reverberated off the stone walls and surged through the throng of spectators.

There, amidst the sea of revelers—gamblers, miscreants, lords in disguise—stood the ring, a square of rope and wood that was both a stage and a gallows. It was there that Darcy "the Dublin Destroyer" O'Dowd, childhood friend and confidant, would fight not just for coin, but for his honor amidst the whispers and lies.

The fact that he was still under suspicion for Vivienne's murder was in no way a deterrent to the evening's spectators. In fact, I thought her death had drawn more interest in the match. Now, Darcy was an upstart who may have used his violent Irish ways on one of London's most beloved society scandals.

They knew nothing of the truth, and in that moment, it was difficult not to hate them for it.

A hush fell over the crowd as the two fighters stepped into the ring. I could scarcely draw breath, sickened by my own voyeuristic thrill even as my eyes devoured Darcy's powerful form.

He climbed into the ring, the muscles of his back coiling beneath his skin, every sinew taut with the readiness of a predator. He caught my gaze for a fleeting moment, his eyes alight with a fire that spoke of more than just determination—perhaps desperation. His opponent, Lewis, loomed opposite, his own frame hewn from relentless toil and strife, his glare unwavering as he faced Darcy across the creaking planks.

The bell's toll, a harbinger of violence, reverberated against the dank walls, mingling with the scent of blood and anticipation. I pressed closer to the ring, my heart thrumming in tandem with the collective pulse of the crowd—a cacophony of cheers and jeers that swelled like a living entity, hungry for the spectacle of brutality. It was a sea of faces awash with excitement and bloodlust, eyes wide, teeth bared in savage delight.

"Come on, punch the Irish git!" a brawny man bellowed beside me, spittle flying from his lips as he thrust a clenched fist into the air.

"Knock his bloody head off, Lewis!" another voice roared from behind, the words laced with a fervor that bordered on fanaticism.

As the first punch was thrown, a visceral connection between combatants and spectators ignited. I flinched at the sound, so raw and primordial—the sickening thud of flesh meeting flesh, an echo of the very pulse of this shadowed underworld. Darcy's fist found its mark on Lewis's jaw, creating an audible crack that sent a collective shiver through the crowd, a wave of energy that fed back into the ring.

A roar exploded from the crowd as the two fighters

collided. Darcy was merciless, unleashing a barrage of punishing blows. The crack of his fists meeting flesh turned my stomach even as I silently urged him on. Blood sprayed, sweat flew, the crowd screamed for more. And there, in the midst of the frenzy, stood Darcy—brutal, dominant, magnificent.

An Irish champion worthy of the name.

"Fight, you milksop! Fight!" a woman screamed with a ferocity that belied her delicate appearance, her bonnet askew as she leapt to her feet, consumed by the frenzy.

I watched, rapt, as Darcy and Lewis circled each other like feral creatures, their bodies slick with sweat that caught the dim light—gladiators in a dance of death. With every jab and hook, every gasp and grunt of exertion, I felt myself drawn tighter into the web of violence woven within these walls. Blood sprayed, a stark crimson against the sawdust, painting a tale of pain and perseverance.

The fight was savage, primal. With each crushing blow, the crowd's bloodlust grew. They bayed and screamed, demanding more violence.

In the midst of this carnival of carnage, I recognized the stoic silhouette of Jorah, his arms crossed as he leaned against a shadowed column—his eyes not on the fight but surveying the crowd, as if he were searching for prey among the predators. Beside him, George Tunstall watched the ring intently, his brow furrowed with a concentration that belied his vested interest in the outcome—a lover's heart beat in tandem with his beloved's fists.

A flash of gold caught my attention, and there, like a gilded statue come to life, stood Clarissa Fairchild. Her elegant poise was a stark contrast to the brutish revelry around her, and yet her eyes gleamed with a cold fascination, a cruel reminder of how closely intertwined high society was with the basest of human desires.

Nearby, Oswald J. Drumft's thick Prussian accent cut through the din as he placed wagers with reckless abandon, his laughter booming like cannon fire. His hunger for victory was palpable, a reflection of his ruthless nature that made men wealthy and graves full.

And there, amidst the cacophony, stood Detective Grayson Croft. His presence was a silent sentinel, his keen eyes dissecting more than the mere spectacle of the fight. A guardian amidst wolves, his grim determination was a beacon to my own, a shared quest that bound us in purpose, if not in heart.

I gazed at him for a moment, and the rest of the world fell away.

Some of the bleakness dulling his vibrant eyes was my fault. As was the slope of his square shoulder, bowed ever so slightly in grief.

How much did he hate me now, for trying to keep this pain away from him?

How much of his fury did I deserve?

A roar drew my notice back to the ring. Darcy was relentless, stalking his opponent, chasing him around the ring. By now, the London Lion could barely raise his guard, overwhelmed by the Dublin Destroyer's onslaught.

A server appeared at my side proffering a glass of deep ruby port.

"Oh, no thank you," I yelled over the din. "I didn't order a drink."

"Compliments of the gentleman, miss." He pointed in the direction of the crowing crowd, his aim hitting one of any dozen strangers.

None of them gentleman by appearance.

"Oh. Well... Thank you." I accepted it with murmured thanks, relieved to wet my parched throat. As my fingers closed around the glass, they brushed a slip of paper folded discreetly against it. I slid the note from the glass and palmed it swiftly. It carried a weight far heavier than its physical presence, and as I unfurled the crisp fold, a chill slithered down my spine, as though the reaper himself had whispered my name.

The slanting script was instantly familiar, conjuring a wash of dread. The message was brief and chilling:

Enjoy the blood sport, my pet. But do not forget who allows you lead rein. Remember what happens to women who sell themselves.

I crumpled the note in my fist, pulse racing.

The Ripper.

He loved to send me letters. To tell me what to do.

How dare he threaten me here? I searched the crowd for a face to match the menacing words, but found only a blur of unfamiliar features. He was playing with me, taunting me.

I wanted to scream in frustration. But I would not give him the satisfaction. I straightened my spine and lifted my chin, refusing to cower before his mind games. The next move was mine.

I forced myself to focus on the spectacle at hand, though my thoughts churned like the stormy Thames. Darcy and his opponent circled each other warily in the ring, their powerful bodies coiled as they fought for breath after a temporary respite between rounds.

At the bell, they collided with the force of rampaging stallions. Darcy's fists hammered his opponent's ribs with sickening thuds. Blood sprayed from the man's smashed nose. The crowd's screams battered my ears as fiercely as the blows battering the fighters.

Sensing the mob's impatience, Darcy moved in for the kill. He unleashed a final devastating combo—left hook, right uppercut, left hook again. His opponent crashed limply to the canvas.

The bell clanged. Darcy raised his fists and bellowed in triumph.

The crowd erupted in a frenzy of fury. Their champion had been defeated.

Darcy didn't need their adulation. He had victory to keep him warm.

I let out a shaky breath, too disturbed by the note burning in my fist to remember my initial thrill at the primal spectacle.

I searched the familiar faces yelling encouragement to Darcy.

Jorah stood surrounded by sycophants and Syndicate, cold but triumphant calculation in his flinty eyes.

Baron and Baroness Morton looked on with aristocratic disdain, though their cheeks were flushed with excitement.

Drumft leered drunkenly, waving fistfuls of banknotes he'd won playing both sides.

Only Tunstall watched with a somber air, his handsome face drawn with concern. Our eyes met briefly across the seething crowd. In them, I saw mirrored my own dread that events were spiraling beyond our control.

The final bell tolled. Darcy stood victorious, chest heaving, blood and sweat mingling in crimson rivulets down his straining body.

The crowd exploded in savage cacophony.

But I felt only the chill of the Ripper's threat creeping down my spine. However this night ended, I sensed the bloody hand of Jack the Ripper lurking behind the scenes, preparing to pull the strings tighter around my throat. I steeled myself to confront the gathering darkness, though it might mean my end.

"Concentrate, Fiona," I whispered through gritted teeth, an attempt to anchor my thoughts away from the Ripper's forbidding message. But the ink of his words was like poison, spreading its tendrils through my mind, leaving me gasping for air amidst the stench of sweat and blood.

He was watching me, even now.

The swell of victory swept through the arena in a deafening roar. Bodies crushed against me, carried by the riptide of excitement. I struggled against the crush, panic rising in my throat. The world tilted, a kaleidoscope of leering faces and flailing limbs.

A heavy blow knocked me to my knees, and no matter how hard I struggled to regain my footing, the press of the crowd kept me down. Heavy boots trampled my dark skirts, pinning me. They tromped on my fingers while their knees knocked into me. I clutched my head, willing my senses to steady, but the ground pitched like a storm-tossed ship.

Jack the Ripper's threat echoed through my mind, the scream of the crowd distorting into a demonic cacophony that threatened to swallow me whole.

A hand grasped my arm. I recoiled, certain the Ripper had come for me at last. But instead of a knife, I felt strong arms encircle me, pulling me close against a solid chest. The clean scent of leather and spice cut through the miasma of blood and sweat.

"Fiona."

Night Horse. His deep voice smooth and cool against my cheek. I clung to him, anchoring myself against the chaos as he stood as my bulwark against the mob. I held tight, loath to leave the shelter of his embrace.

"Can't...breathe," I managed, each word a battle fought against the vise of panic.

"I'll get you out." Night Horse kept one arm firmly around my waist as he guided me through the dispersing throng. I leaned into him, drawing strength from his powerful frame. Amidst the gathering shadows, he was my flicker of light in the darkness. The clamor of the arena receded as Night Horse steered me through the labyrinth of bodies, his hand an unyielding clamp on my waist. We emerged into the cooler air of the London night, a merciful reprieve from the stifling heat and the fetid stench of blood and sweat that permeated the fighting pits. My lungs strained for clean breath, drawing in the damp chill that hung over the city like a shroud.

I gulped lungsful of it, willing my frayed nerves to settle.

"Easy now," he murmured, his voice a steadying thrum against the riot that still sought to invade my senses from behind the heavy doors. "You're safe."

"Safe," I echoed, the word sounding foreign on my tongue as we paused beneath the scant shelter of a crooked awning. The shadows loomed around us, thick with secrets and the whispers of unsavory deeds. Yet here, beside this man—a predator cloaked in human guise—I found an unlikely sanctuary.

"Better?" Night Horse asked, his pale eyes searching my face.

I offered a shaky nod. "Thanks to you. I don't know what came over me in there."

His mouth quirked. "A mob is a deceptively cunning enemy. Even the bravest hearts can falter."

I flushed, grateful for the shadowy alley that hid my burning cheeks. Night Horse thought me brave? Hardly. I was a trembling mess.

"The Ripper found me in there." I unfurled my fist where nervous sweat had dampened the detested letter.

He plucked the paper from my palm and tucked it in a vest pocket before scanning the night in assessment of the few straggling men who'd also sought refuge from the press of humanity inside.

"Lean on me," Night Horse instructed me, his tone imperious yet laced with an undercurrent of concern that belied his austere exterior.

I acquiesced, allowing the weight of my trembling form to rest against his solid presence. His arm was a band of iron around me, fortifying me against the tremors that threatened to usurp my resolve. In this moment of vulnerability, where the specter of the Ripper's warning clawed at my sanity, I clung to Night Horse's strength as if it were the final vestige of hope in a world careening toward oblivion.

"Thank you," I managed to whisper, my voice ragged with gratitude and the remnants of fear. "For... for everything."

"Your gratitude is unnecessary," he replied, scanning the darkened alleyways with a vigilance that bespoke his constant readiness for threat. "It isn't difficult for me to protect you."

I hadn't the strength to feel the surge of emotion that overwhelmed me.

"Even from phantoms?" I asked, half in jest, half desperate to believe in the possibility of being shielded from the terrors that haunted me.

"Especially from them," he said, and there was a glint of something fierce, something indomitable, in his eyes when he looked down at me, but neither of us could conjure a thing to say.

We wound through a maze of narrow lanes, our footfalls muted on the cobbled streets. Fog swirled around us, muffling the distant sounds of the city. To an observer, we would have seemed two ghosts drifting through the mist.

My thoughts churned as I leaned into Night Horse's sturdy frame. The Ripper's note troubled me deeply. How had he known I was at the fight tonight? Was he watching me even now, from the shadows?

What would he think of my present company?

I shivered at the thought, pressing closer to Night Horse. I wondered again at his motives as he guided us expertly through the fog. Perhaps he meant only to keep me safe tonight, to deliver me home untouched by the dangers prowling London's streets.

Or perhaps he had another purpose entirely.

My instincts warred within me, torn between hope and fear. I remembered Jorah's warning that Night

Horse's loyalties were his own. Was I a fool to put my trust in this man?

"Where are you taking me?" I ventured, my voice tinged with the trepidation and curiosity that warred within me.

"Somewhere safe. Somewhere...secluded," he replied, the cryptic timbre of his words wrapping around me like the tendrils of ivy on an ancient mausoleum.

We navigated through serpentine alleys, past shadowy figures that flitted in and out of the gaslight's touch like phantoms. Each step with Night Horse was a descent deeper into the unknown—a fall into the abyss where one could be caught or consumed.

At last, we halted before a structure that exuded an air of quiet dignity, its façade both welcoming and inscrutable. Night Horse ushered me inside, and I crossed the threshold into his sanctum, a place few knew and even fewer had seen. The hush of the river outside hummed a somber lullaby, its waters bearing witness to the myriad sins of this city.

"Night Horse...," I began, my voice a ghostly echo in the dimly lit chamber. "Why bring me here?"

"Because it's the one place they wouldn't think to look for you," he said, closing the door with a finality that sent a chill skittering down my spine. "And because I...trust that you will not reveal its location. Even to the Hammer."

His confession hung between us, heavy with implications that stretched beyond the veil of mere words. In the muted glow of lamplight, his eyes held mine, fierce and unwavering. It struck me then—the gravity of where I stood, at the precipice of revelation or ruin.

"Come," He beckoned, holding open the door.

Heart pounding, I stepped across the threshold into the wolf's den.

Chapter Fifteen

The hush of Night Horse's abode enveloped us, a stark contrast to the raucous London streets we'd just abandoned. The dim glow from oil lamps cast dancing shadows upon the walls, which were adorned with landscape paintings that spoke of faraway places and untamed wilderness. I let my gaze wander across the room, pausing at sculptures of creatures both wild and domestic, marveling at their lifelike forms. My heart raced with the thrill of trespassing into forbidden territory, but my curiosity held me captive.

"Forgive me an impertinent question," I began, my voice barely above a whisper, as if the tranquility demanded it, "but how long have you lived here?"

"Long enough," he replied, his voice low and husky as he closed the door behind me. "I rent this place from an admiral in the navy who spends most of his time abroad, exploring the world." He studied my surprise with amusement, his dark eyes reflecting the dance of the cozy flames in the fireplace. "You're wondering how a heathen like me could appreciate such European culture, aren't you?"

My cheeks flushed under his knowing gaze. I had, indeed, been wondering if he appreciated the art of a culture that extinguished his own. I'd assumed his private domain to be something entirely different, and for that, I realized, I was afflicted with more ignorance than I'd unwittingly ascribed to him. "I apologize," I admitted, bowing my head slightly in contrition, chastened by my own bigotry. "I shouldn't have presumed. I hope I didn't offend you with my clumsy tongue."

"You are forgiven," he said, a teasing smile playing at the corners of his lips. "And it is not my experience that your tongue is clumsy."

As I stood in the softly lit room, surrounded by good taste and safety, I fought a softening of my insides as I gazed at him.

He stood close enough to touch.

But the divide between our lives might as well have spanned continents.

Our conversation shifted then as he produced the disturbing note from Jack the Ripper. His fingers traced over the ink as he read aloud the vile threats.

"Who is he to presume he can dictate your life?" Night Horse growled, his anger echoing my own inward obstinance. "He's obsessed with you, Fiona. And obsessions like these are most often deadly for the woman."

"Do you think he knows I'm here?" I asked, a new fear lancing me through.

He shook his head. "I made certain we were not followed."

Only in a presence like his could I believe that. In the collective imagination, the Ripper was a preternatural enigma. Someone capable of almost inhuman feats of violence and torture.

But so was Aramis Night Horse.

"That isn't to say you don't risk much by being here, alone with me. I've lived among Londoners long enough to know the tongues would wag themselves to ruin if you were discovered here."

"Is it different in America?" I asked, seeking solace in the idea of a world where such constraints did not exist.

He made a face. "It is different with *my* people, because we don't only fuck those we think we own by right of marriage. Love takes many forms, as does partnership. Men such as Darcy and Tunstall, for example, wouldn't have to hide their love from the law."

Shock rippled through me like a cold wave as Night Horse spoke of Tunstall and Darcy's dangerous secret. "How did you find out?" I asked, my voice barely a whisper.

"I figured it out on my own," he replied, his dark

eyes steady and unapologetic. "They're careful, but not as careful as they think."

"Why didn't you ever mention it?" I couldn't hide the surprise in my voice.

"It was irrelevant." He leaned back against a carved wooden chair, the shadows accentuating the strong lines of his face. "Among my people, we know the spirits choose their vessels without regard for the shapes they wear," he continued. "A soul's companion is not bounded by the flesh that cloaks it. If people want to share a home and a bed, there is no reason not to do so. If a woman says she is a man, she may live as a man. Take a wife. Hunt and fight.

"If a man says he is a woman, he may live as a woman. Help sisters, aunts, and cousins raise and teach their children. Weave textiles, trap, and gather. There are no laws to stifle or punish desire and personal truths. We don't have thousand-year-old books to tell us who to fuck and how to behave."

I mulled over his words, feeling the weight of societal expectations pressing down upon me like an iron collar. "That must be a strange but fantastic way to live," I said, my voice tinged with envy as I imagined a world free from the suffocating constraints of society.

Night Horse shifted his gaze toward the window, where the moon cast its pale light across the room. "You seem ready to throw that caution to the wind with Jorah," he observed, his tone inscrutable.

"It was the Ripper that drove me to him, I'm

coming to realize." Heat crept up my cheeks as I recalled my near-encounter with Jorah. "We hadn't actually... Well, we were interrupted before anything transpired... I find myself relieved by the interruption."

He raised an eyebrow. "Why?"

"Because I'm not sure Jorah isn't a monster."

"Be careful of the word 'monster,'" Night Horse warned, his voice somber.

I straightened, sobering at the thought that Night Horse might feel defensive of Jorah. Though the man fancied himself Night Horse's boss in the Syndicate, I always had the notion it was because Night Horse allowed it. And their recent tensions had raised some of my own.

Night Horse was not a leader of men, but an observer of them.

"Why? You don't think the word applies to Jorah?" I asked.

"Because, Fiona," he said, lowering his voice as if to cradle the weight of history, "words have power. They can turn men into monsters, make innocents appear as demons. Even babes turn into baby monsters, needing to be slaughtered before they grow into adult monsters. Such words exist in every language, borne upon the tongues of conquerors. They are legion. They are why I stand before you tribeless. Why some soldier thought my infant son needed to die before he could become a brave."

I closed my eyes, and several monstrous words rose

unbidden to the forefront of my mind. Words that would never wash away, no matter how hard I tried to cleanse my thoughts of them. Words made by other men to oppress and condemn. I wished they didn't live in me.

But they did.

The silence between us grew dense, laden with the unspoken. In the dim light of Night Horse's quarters, our eyes met, and a tacit communion passed between us —a shared understanding born from the ashes of loss.

The words of monsters remained suspended in the air between us, a chilling reminder of the brutality that haunted our pasts. I looked into Night Horse's eyes and saw the same pain that lay buried within my own heart.

We were both survivors, forged in the same fires of anguish and loss.

"Why must empires crush families?" I whispered, as if saying it out loud would make the memories more bearable. "My father and brothers...your wife and child. A million other souls lost, or worse...left behind with the memories of the brutal things we do to each other."

For a moment, we sat in silence, united by the weight of our shared grief. Then, with an unexpected intensity, Night Horse stared deeply into my eyes.

"I still don't know how you look at me," he said, his voice less steady than I'd ever heard it. "Mine was the blade that bled your priest. I know he had gone mad with God, but he was once someone you loved." His eyes held a darkness I'd never seen before, the shadows of regret etched deep within them.

I steeled myself against the resurgence of sorrow, the memory of Aidan's descent into zealotry—a wound that would never heal.

And yet, as a year had gone since the night that Aidan had forced Night Horse's hand, the memory had lost most of its teeth and claws to the truths that were uncovered. "You have nothing to atone for," I assured him, almost meaning it with my whole self. "That man ceased to be the Aidan I knew long before your blade found him. We shall speak no more of it."

Seeking respite from the heaviness, I ventured a question to steer us clear of the shadows. "Are you planning to remain in London long? Bound to Jorah and the Syndicate's designs?" It was something I'd often wondered and never had the guts to ask.

He shrugged, an elegant lift of his broad shoulders. "To be truthful, I never anticipated surviving this long." A wistful smile touched his lips. "Not for lack of trying. With the admiral I spent a few years circumnavigating the globe, and a life at sea was enough to wash the American stink off me. My time with the Syndicate has been...lucrative, as you can see." He motioned to the finery of our surroundings, far surpassing my comfortable, upper-middle-class rowhouse on Tite Street.

"Are you settled here, then?" I queried.

His gaze went to the window, open to allow cool air

to flow over the warmth of the fireplace. A contrast I found delicious on my skin.

"I don't think I'm capable of settling. I am never comfortable, no matter how fine my trappings. I will always be looking for an enemy. I will always return home expecting to find ashes. It is why I would not marry again. I'm too close to a beast to walk this path with a woman, especially a woman of worth."

"How do your people measure worthiness if not by virginity or piety?" I asked, my curiosity piqued. "What is a woman of worth to you?"

"You."

My breath caught, his words igniting something deep within me.

He studied me with an intensity that sent shivers down my spine. "To me, Fiona, you are like an eclipse. Rare. The earth stands still to see but must quickly move on. Your intellect and empathy transfix me. You remind me that I am a man. That you are a woman." He paused, his gaze never leaving mine. "I have worn my weight in chains, Fiona, but you remind me that I was born free. That I used to be like a wolf who could scent entire stories on the breeze. Now I fear I am becoming like Europeans—blind in a windstorm."

The raw honesty of his words stirred something within me, and I felt an unexpected longing for him. Night Horse seemed to sense it too.

He drew closer, his voice dropping to a fervent hush. "We are animals, Fiona. Cloaked in decorum, we feign civility. Yet strip away civilization's veil, and we will bare our teeth over what is ours. I would not presume to own you, to claim you, but I find the instinct to bare my teeth when other men are near."

The weight of his confession hung between us, and in that moment, I saw the man beneath the myth—the soul that yearned for the freedom of open skies and the unfettered howl of the wild.

"I often think of the time I paid for your kiss," he admitted, a tinge of vulnerability lacing his voice. "I find myself craving more."

His confession rendered me speechless, astonishment warring with an arousal that took root deep within my core.

"If Jorah lives in your heart, I'll never speak of this again..." He trailed off, leaving the possibility suspended in the charged atmosphere.

Without a word, driven by an impulse I could neither name nor resist, I leaned forward and pressed my lips to his. The kiss unfolded like the bloom of nightshade—beautiful and dangerous. My pulse quickened, a frantic need driving me, a yearning for connection that bordered on reckless abandon.

I was astonished, yet arousal coursed through my veins, chasing away the remnants of fear the Ripper had provoked in my blood.

I clung to Night Horse like the safety he'd offered. Like my feet were dangling over a precipice only he could pull me away from. As he leaned forward and captured my lips in a breathtaking kiss, my anxiety from the evening fueled a frantic passion.

As I responded with urgency, Night Horse's hands came up to gently capture mine. "Slow down, Fiona," he urged, his touch tender, his tone a soothing balm to my frenzied senses. "There is a saying about slow-burning candles. I forget what it is when you look at me like that."

"There is also something to be said about seizing the day," I replied, my voice quivering slightly, betraying the tempest within me.

Night Horse stared down at me, his dark eyes smoldering with desire. "A day is one rotation of the earth. Then let the earth turn without your having a say about it. Be here with me. Don't seize the moment. Don't hold it too tight. Then it will slip through your fingers like mist. Instead, we can take all day. All night if we want."

His words resonated deep within me, igniting a fire that spread through every inch of my body. As Night Horse's rough hands tenderly traced the curves of my skin, an electric shiver cascaded down my spine. My pulse quickened, and I felt an urgency I'd never known before.

His words, spoken with a native cadence that made them sound like some ancient incantation, washed over me, and I felt myself surrendering to the inevitability of the tide that was drawing us together. I reached for him, sliding my hands across his chest, feeling the heat of his skin beneath the fabric of his shirt. Our lips met again, this time with a hunger that was all-consuming.

"Please...," I whimpered, my body aching for more. He silenced my pleas with a searing kiss, his tongue exploring the depths of my mouth as his hands continued their sinful exploration.

As his mouth moved against mine, I could taste the wildness of him, the untamed spirit that had recognized its counterpart in me. I fumbled with the buttons of his shirt, desperate to feel the reality of him, to confirm that he was not just some fevered dream conjured by my longing.

When the fabric parted, my hands roamed across the landscape of his chest, tracing the scars that spoke of a life marked by violence and survival. He groaned into the kiss, and his hands found their way to the small of my back, pulling me closer until there was no space left between us, until we were pressed so tightly together that I could feel the thrumming of his heart against my own.

Our breaths mingled, hot and fast, as we explored each other with an intensity that bordered on desperation. There was a primal need in his touch, a claiming that spoke of dark nights and even darker passions. His hands traced lower, igniting a trail of fire along my spine that pooled in my belly, coiling tighter and tighter until I thought I might shatter from the intensity of it.

And then his mouth trailed down, following the path his hands had set, leaving a scorching wake across my collarbone and down to the valley between my breasts. With each brush of his lips, each nip and suckle, the world became a blur of sensation, a symphony of pleasure that crescendoed as he continued his descent.

I could feel the roughness of his cheek against the softness of my inner thigh, the hot breath that teased before his tongue delved into the core of my being. It was as if he spoke a language that my body understood innately, answering his every move with a surge of ecstasy that built and built until it broke over me in waves.

I gasped, my voice a keening wail that filled the room as my body convulsed around him, a storm that had been brewing within me finally finding its release.

My fingers tangled in his dark hair as my thoughts spiraled into chaos, consumed by the raw desire that burned between us. As waves of pleasure crashed over me, I surrendered to my first orgasm, my body shuddering with the force of it. In that moment, I felt truly free—free from the constraints of society, free from the suffocating weight of my past, and free to experience the passion that had been ignited by life-affirming danger.

He continued to worship me with his mouth, drawing out every last shudder, every whisper of pleasure, until I lay spent and trembling in his arms. The raw desire that had consumed us both had burned through to something deeper, a connection forged in

the crucible of our shared sorrows and mutual understanding.

As I lay there, panting and dazed, a new awareness
settled over me as heavy as his muscled form. My thighs
cradled his hips, welcomed his sex. It was as if I had
crossed some unseen threshold, stepping out of the
shadows of my past and into a realm where pain and
pleasure, love and loss, were intertwined in an exquisite
tapestry of motion and madness.

Beneath the weight of Aramis Night Horse, the
world turned not just on its axis but spiraled into a
vortex where time and reason lost all meaning. Our
breaths mingled in the dim light as the remnants of our
earlier passion ebbed into a tender dance of interwoven
limbs and shared whispers.

"Does it always feel like this?" I murmured in his
bed some hours later, my voice laden with wonder and
the vestiges of raw need. I traced the lines of his sinewy
arms, feeling the strength that had wielded both
violence and pleasure with equal mastery.

His hands, calloused and unyielding, now roamed
my body with a gentleness that belied their capability
for destruction. In each caress, I found solace—a balm
for wounds unseen but deeply felt.

"I was sure I'd turned to stone," he said, pressing a
kiss to the hollow of my throat, "but your fire... It melts
what it should not."

In the quiet aftermath of our passionate encounter,
I found my senses heightened, acutely aware of every

breath Night Horse took, every whisper-soft touch of his fingers across my flushed skin. Our bodies lay entwined, still trembling from the intensity of our connection.

The remnants of our tempestuous union lingered like the ethereal whispers of fog clinging to the Thames. Night Horse's breath, soft and measured against my temple, was a protection from the storm that had raged within me. Each rise and fall of his chest beneath my cheek was an affirmation—a silent heartbeat syncing with mine.

"Tell me this at least," I murmured, tracing the scars on his chest, each one a hieroglyph of his survival. "Do you ever dream of a different life?"

"Every night," he confessed. "And every morning, I wake to this one."

I lifted my gaze to meet his—those eyes that had seen worlds beyond my ken. The weight of loss shadowed his face, yet in the dim light of his quarters, there flickered something else. Hope, perhaps? Or the glimmer of dreams not yet extinguished?

"Perhaps dreams sustain us more than reality ever could," I offered, and his slight, wistful smile was like the first break in a relentless winter.

"Then may we never wake," he said, cupping my face, brushing my hair back as if he could tuck away the truths we shared along with the stray locks.

"May we never wake," I echoed, leaning into his touch.

We spoke then, not of nightmares, but of the innocence we'd lost—the childhoods stolen by the cruel hands of fate. It was a dance of words and memories, a delicate choreography where pain met comfort, grief met understanding.

I hadn't forgotten about the Ripper's note or any other number of threats and troubles that belonged to me.

But I seized this moment with everything I had.

Because this path may lead me to doom...but my footsteps were finally my own.

Chapter Sixteen

T he disappearing sunlight slanted across the sitting room parquet floor, reaching for the small, toddling form of Tegan. It was a melody I'd come to cherish in the dim corners of my heart. On wobbly legs, the wee thing lurched toward me, her arms outstretched like the branches of an eager sapling reaching for sunlight.

I knelt on the floor, prepared to catch her should she falter.

Mary Sullivan, my housekeeper, clapped her hands from where she stood behind her daughter.

"Look at 'er go, Miss Fiona! Ain't she just the cleverest?" Mary's cockney lilt danced through the air as Tegan plopped into my arms, her giggles infectious and pure.

"Bravo, Tegan!" I exclaimed, the words a rare note of warmth in the otherwise chill room. Mary stood at the edge of the faded Persian rug, clapping her hands, her laughter pealing like church bells through the heavy air of my cozy Chelsea dwelling.

I'd drifted home this morning on sore legs and a cloud of satisfaction, my night with Night Horse a lascivious memory I visited with a secret smile at the most inopportune moments.

He'd been gone when I woke, and I'd dispelled the initial sense of disappointment with the sumptuous breakfast his staff prepared. We'd spoken of what the intimacy meant before we indulged.

Or, rather, what it didn't mean.

What we shouldn't expect.

I'd do well to remember that the man I'd ultimately chosen as a lover was a murderer for hire. A broken man whose heart was buried with his murdered wife and son in a grave on the other side of the Atlantic.

I reminded myself last night was a respite for two weary souls. Nothing more.

And that life was wondrous and weird.

At least *my* life.

"Me little bird's already about to fly the nest." Mary beamed with pride, her round cheeks flushed with the joy that only a mother's love could paint.

She'd not said a word when I arrived home late morning in the same gown I'd left in the night before.

Instead, she'd brewed me a terrible cup of coffee and drawn me a bath.

I'd met Mary at Katherine Riley's murder scene.

The twenty-year-old girl had been recently widowed by a factory accident and had planned to use her husband's last coin to give her baby up to a wealthier couple before she committed herself to the workhouse.

Maybe it was because she looked like my own Mary Kelly, or because I'd just found out that Katherine Riley would have cremated poor Tegan and pocketed Mary's money like she had with Amelia Croft's child. I lied to myself and said it was because I was a decent person...

But I hired Mary on the spot. A woman with exactly no training or knowledge in the art of housekeeping.

To my surprise and delight, she was a quick study and could do the work of two women all with her toddler underfoot.

As a bonus, Aunt Nola had taken to her immediately and been a bit healthier since Tegan's sunny yawps filled our house with enough noise to drown out her ever-present spirit guides and their incessant portents of danger and doom.

"This little wanderer is a natural," I replied, settling Tegan back onto the carpeted surface. The child gazed up at me, her eyes wide and trusting, as though the sordidness that lingered just beyond these walls could never touch her. I envied her blissful ignorance, wished I could shield her from the London that lay in wait—a beast with an insatiable hunger for innocent souls.

"Go on, darling," Mary coaxed, kneeling and stretching out her arms to her daughter. "Show Miss Fiona one more time."

Tegan took a tentative step, then another, her gait growing surer until she reached her mother's embrace. They laughed together, a sound so sweet it almost banished the shadows from my heart.

The moment, however, was shattered as brisk knocks echoed against the oak door, a harbinger of reality's cruel return.

"Stay with her," I instructed Mary, brushing past her as I moved toward the entrance. My heart hammered a familiar rhythm of foreboding against my ribs as I opened the door to reveal a young messenger boy, his cap held in dirty fingers.

"Miss Fiona Mahoney?" he queried, breathless, the urgency in his voice a mirror of my own racing thoughts.

"That's me," I confirmed, my gaze falling to the crumpled paper he extended toward me. Snatching it with a swift motion, I unfolded the note, and the elegant script delivered its grim summons.

A body at the Lyceum. Your expertise required immediately.

No signature adorned the message, but none was needed. I'd recognize Dr. Phillips' tidy script anywhere. There was only one reason my presence would be requested in London's theater district—someone was dead, and it fell upon me to wipe their offal from the stage, as it were.

"Thank you, I'll be there directly," I said, slipping

the boy a coin, which disappeared into his pocket as quickly as he did down the street.

Turning back to the parlor, I caught the last remnants of Tegan's mirth before the mask of my profession settled upon my features.

"Mary," I called, my tone clipped with the gravity of my task. "I must away to the Lyceum. Please send for Hao Long to meet me there."

"Of course, Miss Fiona," she replied, her smile fading as she gathered her daughter close, sensing the shift in the atmosphere.

"Keep the doors locked," I added, a final instruction born of knowing too well the darkness that waited for the last slivers of the day to abate.

※

UPON ARRIVAL, the Lyceum loomed, an edifice of entertainment now tainted by tragedy. Constables and onlookers alike lingered outside, their whispers weaving a tapestry of dread. Stepping past them with a nod, I slipped beneath the velvet rope that served as a barrier to the curious and the craven.

Inside, I found Dr. Phillips near the stage, his countenance grave as he presided over the macabre scene. Constables and detectives had cleared away from the inner scene and the body, making way for the coroner to take it, as usually happened by the time I was called.

They'd be off investigating, giving hardly a thought to the mess death tended to leave behind.

The footlights cast an eerie glow upon the lifeless form of a young woman sprawled like a five-pointed star in a stark white gown. Her beautiful face, now twisted in a grimace of death, bore the marks of violence. Her chestnut hair was a cascade of sorrow upon the wooden boards.

"Miss Mahoney," Dr. Phillips greeted me, tipping his hat in somber respect. "A grim evening we find ourselves in."

"Indeed, doctor," I replied, my gaze never leaving the victim's unblinking one. "What happened?"

"Her name was Lena Goldman. An actress of some renown, and a friend to Vivienne Bloomfield-Smythe, I'm told," Dr. Phillips murmured, swiping off his bowler hat to scratch at his balding pate as he gave me a meaningful look. "Killed in a similar manner, if the dent in the back of her head bears out the suspicion it causes. She's been here for some time, since before noon, I hazard."

Though she'd not been stabbed or shot, there was still blood. It leaked from a nose that had been broken before she'd died. From a mouth missing teeth. Her death was not swift, as Vivienne's had been. Nor was it staged dramatically.

Apart from her being draped across an actual stage.

"Makes one wonder if there is someone with a grudge against actresses in particular." He turned to me

with an imperious scowl. "A most Elizabethan sentiment, Miss Mahoney, wouldn't you agree? Draconian,
even."

"Hmm," I murmured as I studied the body, my
thoughts churning over all the possibilities.

An irate voice echoed through the empty theater,
shrill in its desperation. "Why is no one looking for
her?" a woman cried from behind the velvet rope.
"What if she was taken? What if she done it?"

Dr. Phillips and I watched as the last of the constables ushered her back into the lobby, though she struggled and cursed them the entire way.

"Looking for whom?" I queried. "What is she on
about?"

"Evidently, Miss Goldman had taken on a new
assistant of late—a girl now vanished into the ether, I'm
afraid." He sighed, adjusting his spectacles.

"Vanished?" The word hung between us, fraught
with implications. An assistant fled was a story half
told, secrets locked behind lips now absent. My pulse
thrummed with the urgency of unraveling this latest
knot in our sordid tapestry.

"None among the troupe can account for her whereabouts since the curtain's fall," Dr. Phillips continued.

I absorbed this new wrinkle, my mind already
sifting through possibilities and connections. The
actress angle was a strong one, but my instincts didn't
tend in that direction. Lena's ties to Vivienne could not
be overlooked, nor the enigma of her absent aide.

Combined with the small detail of her surname: Goldman.

She had Jewish heritage.

"Will you send for me if you find anything that connects her to Vivienne's death?" I implored, my voice low. "Any detail may prove crucial."

"Of course," he assured me, before turning to oversee Lena's final exit from the stage she'd once graced.

As Lena's mortal remains were carefully hoisted upon the gurney, a glint among the sawdust and spilt rouge caught my eye—a tiny beacon in the abyssal dark. I knelt, brushing my fingers against the cold, metallic surface of a gold charm. An oak leaf, delicate and solitary, lay in stark contrast to the bloodstained wood beneath it.

"Doctor, look here," I called out, gingerly lifting the object from its resting place.

"Curious," Dr. Phillips said, leaning closer. His brow furrowed as he inspected the charm. "An adornment, perhaps, for a high collar. But whether it graced a man or woman, that remains uncertain."

"Who is the detective on this case?" I asked.

"Why, it's Croft, of course. His second since he was nicked from Whitechapel to work at the main office of Scotland Yard. Our boy is doing well, wouldn't you say? Though he seemed to have scampered away since I called for you."

At the mention of Croft, my heart fell into my stomach and the world tilted a little.

Would that it was anyone but him.

At least he hadn't mentioned to Dr. Phillips the reason for his temper at me.

"It could be nothing but a piece of costume frippery," I suggested, frustration lacing my words. The golden leaf seemed to pulse with significance—some vital clue—even before Dr. Phillips validated my suspicion.

"That's no bit of costume jewelry, Miss Mahoney," he surmised, itching at his scruff. "That's pure gold if I've ever seen it. If I were you, I'd run it by Croft's desk to be sure." He nudged me with his sharp elbow as he twitched bushy eyebrows in my direction. "He likes the days he gets to look at you, even if he shows his teeth sometimes."

A bleak wound opened in my soul as I realized that Croft would no longer treat me with his signature form of gruff acquiescence and protective disapproval. I'd wounded him in kind and betrayed his beloved sister.

I couldn't decide if I wished I'd told him the truth the moment I found it or if I should have kept the secret forever.

"Take it with you, Fiona," Dr. Phillips advised, his voice solemn. "Scotland Yard might glean something we cannot."

"Indeed," I replied, the weight of the charm heavy

in my palm. "Farewell, doctor. Your work is not envied this night."

"Nor yours," he returned, his gaze holding mine with a gravity that spoke of shared burdens, shared resolve, before he tipped his hat to me and went on his way.

Left alone in the wake of the departed, I searched the void of the empty and unlit audience—a Stygian chasm too terrifying for me to contemplate.

How did they do it night after night, stare into the darkness and recite their lines? Use their limbs and words to tell someone else's story. To embody another so well, the audience believed you were they.

Since Hao Long had yet to arrive with my cart, and Dr. Phillips was clearing the stage for my work, I navigated through the hushed murmurs and discreet sobs of gathered onlookers. My wandering led me to the lobby, where the outspoken theater employee stood cloaked in mourning, her eyes rimmed red with recent tears.

"Miss?" I ventured, my voice tempered with reverence for the fallen. "I heard you mention that Miss Goldman's assistant is missing."

The woman lifted her gaze, fraught with sorrow and suspicion. "Who wants to know?"

"I'm Fiona Mahoney. I'm an...associate to Dr. Phillips, the coroner." Not a lie, though not a spectacular truth, either.

"Eliza," she replied, offering her hand, which I shook.

"You said Lena's maid is missing?"

"She's disappeared. No one has seen hide nor hair since dusk fell. The detective said he'd look for her, but never even asked where poor Claudia lived or what she looked like. How would he even know?"

The name hit me like a sledgehammer to the middle.

"Did you say her assistant's name was Claudia?"

Eliza nodded, lips pulled tight with strain. "Lena was well proud of 'er. Used to work for the one and only Vivienne Bloomfield-Smythe before she—" The girl's eyes widened to the extent I worried they'd pop right out of her head. "Now both actresses she worked for are murdered. Which means either she did it. Or..."

Eliza was apparently no fool, already seeing the threads that might weave this grim tapestry together.

Claudia was very likely victim or villain.

"Was Claudia getting along here?" I asked.

"Well enough for the couple days she had," the actress replied, a shiver passing through her slender frame. "She was a mousy little mite. Didn't say much. But Lena trusted Claudia implicitly. She was impressed by her...fervent loyalty to Vivienne, even after her death. I always thought it a little—touched, if you ask me."

"Obsession often masquerades as loyalty," I mused, a chill skimming down my spine at the thought of Claudia's intense fixation. Could she have turned it on Lena?

"There's more." Eliza leaned in, voice low enough for a confessional. "Lena... She was to meet with a gentleman after the final curtain—she kept his name shrouded in mystery, even from us."

"Did she now?" My own voice was a wisp of smoke, dissipating into the cold air. "Did you reveal that to the detectives?" I watched her closely, searching for a flicker of insight within those pools of earnest fear.

"The big one said that without a name or a place it was impossible to know who, but he'd ask around in case someone else was told a name," she replied, shaking her head with a conviction that surprised me. "But Lena wouldn't tell nobody if she found a rich keeper. Not until she'd cemented a contract or something."

"Thank you for your information—it's been most helpful," I said. "And please be careful to look out for yourself."

With the gold oak leaf charm hidden away, I resolved to confront Detective Grayson Croft. He was a man of stern constitution, his edges roughened by the relentless grind of seeking truth amid the city's ever-twisting labyrinth of lies.

But he was good at what he did. Scotland Yard promoted only the best detectives to work at their coveted main offices and on such high-profile cases.

Amelia must be so pleased with him.

As I stepped out into the fog-shrouded streets of London, the cold tendrils of mist licked at my skin like icy serpents, as though they, too, sought to uncover the secrets hidden within the city's shadows. The gold charm weighed heavily in my pocket, a constant reminder of the task that lay before me. I ventured forth into the night, the echo of my footsteps a lonely dirge for justice yet unserved, until I found myself beneath the stone façade of Scotland Yard.

I hastened up the steps. A fleeting glimpse of Detective Croft disappearing into the bowels of that stone edifice spurred me onward.

"Detective Croft!" The words tumbled from my lips with fervent urgency as I approached the desk sergeant, a man whose face was as worn as the ledger he toiled over.

"May I assist you, madam?"

"I need to speak with Detective Croft. Now." I leaned forward. "Please tell him Miss Fiona Mahoney has uncovered evidence in the Lena Goldman case." I didn't want to say Vivienne's ultra-recognizable name in a room full of people.

The sergeant cast a dubious glance toward the corridor Croft had taken. "Wait here," he grumbled, and vanished into the shadows beyond.

Moments stretched into eons, each second weighted with the gravity of the evidence burning a hole in my pocket. When the sergeant reemerged, his expression bore ill news.

"Detective Croft is not in the building," he announced, the finality in his tone brooking no argument.

"Impossible! I saw him enter not moments ago," I

protested, the heat rising in my cheeks. "I have compelling evidence—"

"Leave it with me," he interrupted, hand outstretched, palm upturned and expectant.

My body trembled with rage, my fists clenching so hard that my nails dug into my palms. How dare Croft ignore me out of spite? I could feel my blood boiling as I stormed away from him, each step on the marble floor echoing like a thunderous drumbeat. Fine—if he wanted to play games, I'd find another way to get him the information, but I didn't dare trust it in the hands of just anyone.

When I dashed back into the street, nightfall drew its cloak tighter around the city. And in its embrace, I resolved to seek out Aramis Night Horse, convinced that only he could navigate the treacherous waters that now threatened to engulf me, and if not, he'd at least use his considerable resourcefulness to help.

The Velvet Glove was only a handful of blocks from Scotland Yard, a location that seemed as natural to me as it was strange.

The fog hung thick and low over the streets, a spectral shroud that seemed to whisper of the city's hidden sins. I hastened through the murky veil, my thoughts on Night Horse, his shadowy presence promising both knowledge and peril.

Perhaps pleasure.

The damp cobblestones of the Strand whispered secrets beneath my hurried steps, a sibilant symphony to accompany the tumult of my thoughts. The night air clung to me, heavy with the promise of rain and the electric scent of imminent revelations.

It was in this murky twilight that she appeared. Claudia, Vivienne's shadow, slipping from the veil of fog like a specter summoned by my own troubled musings.

"Miss Mahoney." Her voice was a tight thread fraying at the edges. "I must speak with you—in private."

My heart quickened as I eyed her warily. "Claudia? Are you all right? Everyone thinks you've been taken, or worse. Do you know what happened to Lena?"

I might have been more circumspect if she'd not startled me so thoroughly, but my mouth ran away before my wits could catch them up.

Her eyes darted about, seeking refuge in the shadows that enveloped us. "It's not safe out here. Please, come with me to the Velvet Glove."

I relaxed a little, knowing that our journeys had the same destination tonight.

A shiver traipsed down my spine, not from the chill but from the clandestine urgency in her tone. "Claudia, you have to tell me, do you know anything about Lena or Vivienne's murders? Do you think they are connected?" I pressed, inching closer, my senses sharpening to the hidden nuances of her demeanor. Had she been the one to bash both their heads in from behind?

Seeing her slight form now, it was hard to believe.

Still, I wouldn't be allowing her behind me anytime soon.

Claudia hesitated, a delicate tremor in her lips betraying the fear that gripped her. "They knew each other... But that's not important now."

"Then enlighten me," I urged, "to what is important."

She leaned in, her breath a ghost against my cheek. "I know who killed Vivienne."

I nearly tripped over her confession and had to grasp her arm to keep from sprawling on the walk.

"Tell me," I said softly, sensing the brittle edge of trust that held her confession aloft.

Her gaze flitted to mine. "I can't," she whispered, looking up at me as if to apologize for her most egregious sin. "I'm sorry," she whispered.

"You don't have to be," I said, stopping to clasp both of her freezing hands in mine. "My only interest in this case is justice for Vivienne, and to clear Darcy's name. Surely you don't want an innocent man to hang for her death?"

Casting her frantic gaze about, she found a tight alley and pulled me away from the unceasing shine of the Strand. "I'm so afraid," she confessed.

"I know." I huddled in tight, hoping to protect her from the darkness beyond. "I will stay with you, Claudia," I promised. "We will take the information to the men who have the power to avenge her death. Don't you want to do that for Vivienne?"

Her wide eyes never blinked as they filled with moisture, gleaming up at me with that worshipful gaze that
broke my heart.

"I'm sorry," she whispered. "I'm so sorry."

My question was taken by an explosion of pain that
stole my vision.

And then my consciousness.

Chapter Seventeen

Consciousness crept back to me like a sinister shadow, crawling across the cobwebs of my mind. A dull ache throbbed at the base of my skull, a cruel reminder of the violence that had brought me to this dire circumstance. I stirred, only to find my movements restricted, bonds tight around my wrists and ankles, tethering me to a cold, unyielding chair. Panic's icy fingers clawed at my chest as I strained against the ropes, desperation lending me futile strength.

A chill swept over me, colder than the grave, and it wasn't solely from the dank air. The foul stench of the river invaded my nostrils, decay and brine that one could never forget, mingling with the copper scent of spilled blood. My heart stuttered, but a morbid curiosity urged my eyes to adjust quicker to this infernal gloom.

Immediately I wished to return to the bliss of unconsciousness.

Because I saw her—a shapeless form sprawled upon the floor mere inches from my bound feet. My breath hitched as the details coalesced into a dreadful truth.

Claudia, Vivienne's shadow turned specter, lay motionless, the pallor of death stealing the manic gleam once ever-present in her eyes.

A whimper escaped me.

I strained against the chair, seeking any telltale sign of where I might be held captive. The edges of my world were blurred, yet through the shadows emerged the stark outline of a warehouse. Brick and concrete, cold and unyielding, much like the corpse at my feet.

The horror of it all threatened to unleash the bile rising in my throat. Claudia had summoned me into the alley, distracted me so my stealthy assailant could clobber me over the head. She'd trusted whoever was behind this. That gullible, hopeful fixation, that all-consuming adoration she harbored for Vivienne—and possibly my attacker—had been her undoing, leading to her grim fate.

But there was no time for sorrow or revulsion; such luxuries were afforded to those far removed from the clutches of malevolence. My mind, ever my weapon, sharpened itself against the whetstone of necessity. There must be a weakness—a loosened rope, a forgotten tool of escape, anything to exploit. With each tentative shuffle, each careful twist of my wrist, I sought my salvation in the oppressive gloom.

"Think, Fiona," I chided myself, grappling for that sliver of cunning that had kept me alive all this time on my own. My mind raced, each thought a spark in the dark, seeking a way out. I wasn't done with this life. Too many people needed me.

Mary's memory needed me.

"Hello?" The question was a whisper to the dead, to the ghosts that lingered in the corners of this godforsaken place. To whoever had tied me up. "Who are you?" I was proud that emerged as a demand, at least.

No answer echoed back from beyond the gloom.

Could Jack the Ripper have found me? Could this be his punishment for the hours spent in Aramis Night Horse's bed?

The reek of iron and despair hung heavy in the air, a tangible curtain of dread. Yet beneath it lingered something else—a scent almost lost to the olfactory din. The faint, familiar tang of chemicals used in my postmortem sanitation work teased at my senses. Ammonium hypochlorite. Sodium bismuth. Creosote? It held a twisted irony, that the very agents used to erase the evidence of death might well be my key to life.

Though my senses were sharp from fear, I could see very little, and had no clue from which direction the scents originated.

It wasn't the first time in my life I'd been bound, but

I couldn't remember ever feeling so frightened. So certain that I was closer to death than I'd ever been. Close enough to shake his hand.

Perhaps even steal a kiss.

The staccato rhythm of approaching footsteps resonated against the cold stone. I strained against the darkness, but its oppressive weight bore down on me like the lid of a coffin.

Shadows coalesced into the form of a man, and Oswald Drumft emerged from the dimness like a specter born of my most harrowing nightmares. His eyes, frostbitten chips of disdain, locked on to me with a predator's focus—a raptor eyeing its next kill.

"Fiona Mahoney. For a name that holds no political strength, no family fortune, no nobility or great accomplishments, it is certainly spoken often in the halls of power." Drumft's voice slithered through the darkness, and the devil's glare examined me like I were a stain he needed to wipe off his shoe. "I find it arouses me that fear tarnishes your otherwise defiant visage."

I fixed him with a steely gaze, one honed by years of hiding my true self beneath layers of necessary deception.

"Is it fear you see, Herr Drumft?" My voice was steadier than I felt, the words wielded like blades. "Or perhaps it is disgust for the man who boasts of his conquests in and out of the bedroom, yet trembles in the presence of real men?"

His eyes flared, and fleshy, ever-damp lips parted in a maniacal smile. "Fear?" he echoed, drawing out the word like a caress, "Women are but trifles, Miss Mahoney. True power lies in subjugation. There is no man nor woman on this isle who holds power over me, but I delight in bending the will of others to my own desires."

"Desires," I spat, tasting the venom in it, "born from what? A hunger for control? A deep-seated loathing for yourself and your monstrous deeds? There's a place in hell for men like you, Drumft, and you'll be sent there soon enough."

"Monstrous?" His laugh was devoid of mirth, a hollow sound that reverberated off the stark walls. "You speak of monsters, yet you work for the Syndicate."

"Not by choice," I hissed, deciding I would not use what might be my final words to explain myself to the likes of him. "Vivienne, Lena, Claudia. How many other women have you crushed beneath your boot?"

His lips twisted into a grotesque semblance of pride. He circled me, a predator reveling in the scent of terror, each footfall a measured torment. "Vivienne had convinced me she was a perfect flower in my garden, when in fact she was a weed. Fodder for vermin, to be rooted out and exterminated. As for Lena... Yes, well, she was a necessary sacrifice. England must purge itself of filth, mustn't it?"

I held fast to the steel within my soul. If survival

demanded a chess match with the devil himself, then let the game begin. For every move he plotted, I vowed to counter; for every horror he promised, I would rise indomitable. In this dance macabre, I was no mere pawn—he would find the queen had teeth.

"You truly are a cretinous creature!" I cried.

"Flattery will get you everywhere, dear Fiona." His leer deepened. "Now, I heard whispers that you were at Scotland Yard claiming that you'd retrieved something from the theater where I left Lena." He stood at attention before me in his complete diplomatic regalia, his high collar sporting a gold oak pin on the left of his throat as if to advertise the absence of the right.

Why did a Prussian diplomat have ties in Scotland Yard?

My mind raced as panic gnawed at my resolve. The pin, a symbol of his rank and sin, was indeed in my possession—the one thing that could place him at the scene of Lena's murder. "If I give it to you," I said, desperation seeping into my tone, "will you let me go?"

"Let you go?" A laugh, dark and forbidding, erupted from him. "Oh, no, my dear. Whether you return it or not, you will die. If you produce the pin, I'll be merciful. If you are prone to defiance, well... Your end will not be as swift as Vivienne's, nor as merciful as Lena's."

I glimpsed movement behind him: a shadow detaching from darkness, forming into the shape of a man—his lackey.

"Dieter here will see to that," Drumft said, nodding toward the hulking figure who stepped forward, a glint of metal in his hand.

I searched the recesses of my terrified mind, frantically clawing for an inkling of a plan. My life, a threadbare tapestry of loss and vengeance, depended on the cunning that had saved me more times than I dared count.

"Think carefully, Miss Mahoney," he continued. "Your silence could be...detrimental to more than just your own fragile existence."

His words were calculated, designed to pry into the crevices of my resolve. Yet my thoughts flitted to the others who might be ensnared by his vile machinations, or already had been—Darcy, Jorah, Croft, Aunt Nola, Mary, and even baby Tegan. Was this man a threat to them all?

"Your threats are as empty as your soul, Drumft," I retorted, though the effort cost me a tremor in my voice I could ill afford. A lie, albeit a necessary one; his threats were far from empty, and we both knew it.

"Bravery or foolishness?" he mused aloud, his footsteps a measured patrol on the cold stone floor. "I wonder which you possess in greater measure."

"Perhaps," I said, "it is not terror that moves my tongue but a resolve you cannot fathom."

He laughed—a low, guttural sound devoid of humor—and the room seemed to constrict around us. "Very well," he growled, moving closer until I could feel the heat of his breath. "Your tenacity will be your undoing, Miss Mahoney. I shall enjoy breaking it."

His presence loomed over me, oppressive and unyielding. Yet even as the threat of pain closed in like a storm cloud ready to burst, my mind scoured the situation for any sliver of advantage. Anything that could be turned against him, any oversight on his part that I might exploit.

"Break me, then," I challenged, mustering the remnants of my courage. "But know this—you may force me to bend, yet I shall never truly be at your mercy."

"I am not without Mercy, Fiona," he said. "But Dieter here has none."

Dieter was not so large as Croft, tall as Jorah, or lethal as Night Horse, but he was some Prussian amalgamation of all these traits beneath a perfectly pomaded light head of hair. He looked through me, as if his dark deeds were already done, and I was the rubbish left leaking after.

My gaze ricocheted to the very edges of where the light touched the echoing, empty chamber, desperately seeking something, anything, that might offer me a shred of hope. It danced over the grainy textures of brick and mortar, the vague shadows cast by the feeble light struggling to penetrate the dense air, before finally settling on a pile of detritus in the corner. An ember of resolve kindled within my chest. A weapon could be hidden there. Perhaps my salvation.

"Your eyes betray you, Miss Mahoney." Drumft's voice cut through the haze of my thoughts, as cold and sharp as a knife's edge. "Seeking your escape? Futile."

"Escape?" I echoed with feigned innocence. "Why would I flee from such charming company?"

"Charming," he scoffed, stepping closer, dropping his voice to a vile whisper. "You are too common for my bed, Fiona. Too educated for your own good. The Irish taint in your blood is almost as repulsive as that of the Jews."

I swallowed hard against the bile rising in my throat. His words were like acid, corroding the very air between us. But I couldn't afford to recoil, not even from this. "Truly, that was why you killed Vivienne?" I asked, my voice steady despite the tremor in my soul. "Because she was born a Jew?"

"Vivienne was born a mistake," he spat. "A beautiful lie that concealed filth. She allowed me to sully myself with her impure blood." His disdain twisted into a grotesque smile. "Lena, on the other hand, was but a pawn, lured by coin, yet I never sullied my hand with touching her. A fate far less than she deserved."

"Such mercy," I murmured, the irony bitter on my tongue.

"Mercy?" He laughed. "Their kind does not deserve mercy."

"What about Claudia?" I pressed, needing to understand the full measure of his depravity.

"You mean Claudia *Frenkel* here? Her father is a rabbi." He sneered down at her, and I had the abrupt impulse to shield her body from his disrespectful gaze. "Blackmailed to betray her mistress, then coerced into servitude," he said with casual brutality. "Her fate was sealed from the start."

His confession was a serrated blade to my heart. Claudia, whose only crime was being born. I'd assumed her surname was shared with the family she'd been staying with. Instead, she'd shared initials with a crucial piece of evidence found at a murder scene—and it had occurred to no one she might have been clever enough to change her name.

Because she was the serving class.

I didn't have time to wallow in my shame, but I felt it, deeply.

In the suffocating darkness, a feeble spark of hope flickered to life within me. By some fortuitous twist of fate, my trembling fingers brushed against a knot in the ropes—a loose, careless thing. It seemed almost a mockery of my dire predicament, but I latched on to it as though it were a lifeline cast into stormy seas. With each delicate tug, I willed the fibers to yield, praying for the shadows to cloak my desperate endeavor.

"Come now, Fiona." Drumft's voice slithered through the gloom. "You must realize the futility of your situation. The sooner you give me what I want, the sooner any unpleasantness will be over." He nodded to Dieter, who wouldn't stop looking at my hair as he approached. "Dieter will first cut away your clothing to search it...then we will begin searching your body for hiding places."

I ignored Drumft's taunting, focusing instead on the slow give of the rope. If courage had a taste, it was the metallic tang of fear mingled with resolve upon my tongue.

"Please," I began, my voice breaking as I let the mask of composure slip. Granted, my fear wasn't entirely acted, as there was plenty of panic surging through my blood to draw from. Tears welled in my eyes, spilling over as I sobbed and begged for mercy. "Please, don't do this."

The ropes had slackened enough for me to use the sweat to slide my little finger free, then a second one, a silent victory in the oppressive darkness. But before I could dream of unfettered wrists, Dieter towered over me.

"Begging suits you, Fiona," Drumft sneered, relishing my apparent despair. "But you should have given me what I asked for before I had to deploy Dieter."

I dropped my head as if in defeat.

"And you...should have tied my feet."

I lashed out as swiftly as I could, the sharp toe of my day boot connecting audibly with Dieter's shin bone. He yelped a German curse word and back-handed me with such force, I tipped over, chair and all.

The impact of my landing rattled my teeth and stole my breath.

But it also broke the rickety chair.

The last vestiges of my feigned sobs turned to grunts of exertion, and my fingers, slick with perspiration and fear, grasped at the jagged wood.

"Pathetic," Drumft spat, watching with twisted amusement that soon faltered as the ropes binding me slackened. The fibers that had bit into my wrists gave way, and the coarse threads fell from my chafed skin.

Instinct took the reins as I ducked away from Drumft's grasp, scrambling to hoist the chair between me and them like a lion tamer in a circus tent. His fingers clawed at the air where I had been moments before, his anger a palpable force.

I ignored the throbbing pain, the sting of raw flesh, letting the surge of adrenaline sharpen my focus. I was not just Fiona Mahoney, crime scene cleaner, nor merely an immigrant shadowed by sorrow—I was survival incarnate, fueled by the memory of each soul unjustly taken and every secret buried by cruel, self-important men like him.

Drumft's face contorted with fury as his prey turned predator. With a guttural roar, he hurled himself at me, his bulk a weapon forged from malice and brute force. But I was no longer the woman tied to a chair; I was a tempest unleashed, every lesson from Darcy, every roughhouse tussle with Flynn, every impromptu defense strategy explained by Croft now etched into my very sinew.

Drumft approached head-on, and Dieter had begun to circle to my left, but I remembered the way Darcy would dance around his opponents, the economy of motion, the precision.

I broke away one of the chair's splintered legs and didn't waste time by threatening, instead clubbing Oswald J. Drumft right across his sneering face.

Blood spurted from his nose, a crimson mask that seemed to unleash an even darker demon within him. He howled, more beast than man.

Dieter came at me again, his fingers clawing the air like talons.

With the agility born from years of survival—and perhaps a touch of that iron-willed Irish luck—I feinted to the left and swung hard. The chair leg connected with the side of his knee with a sickening crack, sending him sprawling to the cold concrete floor.

I struck Drumft again, targeting the solar plexus. Darcy's voice echoed in my mind with an image of the day by the River Shannon when he'd taught me to steal Flynn's breath with little more than a tap.

Drumft doubled over, gasping, the sound music amidst the racket of our struggle.

My lungs burned with exertion, the taste of blood and vengeance thick on my tongue.

Dieter had struggled to his feet and loomed before

me, a predator's glint in his eye, but I had been prey for too long. The chair leg felt like an extension of my own furious will as I grasped it, splinters biting into my palm.

"Come closer, and you'll join your master in his misery," I snarled. Dieter hesitated, knife glinting wickedly in the meager light, but his resolve wavered as he saw the determination etched in every line of my being.

I lunged forward, feigning an attack to his face, then pivoted sharply, driving the jagged wood into the soft flesh of his shoulder. To my astonishment, he screamed and stumbled back, clutching at the wound. Seizing the moment, I bolted past him into the dark hallway.

Corridors snaked before me, their crooked angles and diverging paths a dark reflection of the twisted mind that pursued me. Mold-ridden wallpapers clung to the walls like the lingering touch of the damned, and each flickering gaslight threw monstrous shadows that danced with sinister glee. My heart thrummed a frantic rhythm in my chest, the beat punctuated by the distant thunder of footsteps chasing me.

I rounded a corner and stumbled into a narrower passage, feeling the air growing colder, as if kissed by the breath of ghosts. Drumft's pursuit seemed to grow fainter, the distance between us widening with every desperate stride. Yet my soul was not deceived; his malice lingered in the very air, a miasma of hatred and unyielding intent.

The walls were oppressive, the air fetid with decay, but there was a window—a small, taunting promise of freedom high above. It was no more than a sliver of moonlight, but to me, it was a beacon toward life. I looked about the squalid corridor, seeking anything to aid my escape. The window was a cruel mistress, too high to reach without help, but desperation lent clarity to my mind. There, against the wall, lay a stack of crates, abandoned and forgotten.

I scrambled atop the crates, and their wood creaked ominously beneath my weight. Each movement was precise, the result of years spent navigating alleyways and rooftops, fleeing specters of my past. But now, I wasn't running away—I was climbing toward salvation.

"That way! Get her!" Drumft barked, but his lackey was sluggish, the sticky blood soaking through the shoulder of his shirt and jacket no doubt slowing him down. With each second that ticked by, I ascended higher, my fingers finding purchase on the rough brickwork. I could almost taste the fog-laden air of London's freedom as I hoisted myself up, reaching for the window's ledge.

The pile wavered as Dieter reached it and kicked out at the rotting wood, breaking a corner. One more blow and the entire thing would come down.

With a final surge of effort, I wedged my fingers into the narrow opening, pulling with all the strength that anger and hope could muster. The window groaned in protest, a pained symphony to accompany my escape.

Below, Drumft's curses faded into a frustrated echo.

As I hoisted myself up, glass bit into my palms, sharp as the memories that haunted me. But pain was a small price to pay for escape. With a grunt, I squeezed through the opening, and the edges of the window cut into my sides like the harsh words of those who'd doubted I would ever amount to anything more than a poor Irish immigrant.

"See you in hell, Drumft!" I hissed into the void as I pushed through.

I tumbled onto the cobblestones outside, the dampness seeping through my clothes, grounding me in the reality of my escape. I lay there, stunned, for a heartbeat, the mix of fear and triumph, pain and disbelief, coursing through me like a heady elixir.

A racket of masculine voices and footsteps stirred me from where I fought to catch my breath, and by the time I'd summoned the strength to run again, Drumft was pulling the heavy door to the warehouse open, and Dieter was limping after him.

I knew exactly where I was, thankfully, as the landmark of Blackfriar's Rail Bridge grounded me on the serpentine grid of London's streets.

Without stopping, I gathered my skirts to my knees and sprinted with every last ounce of speed I had toward the beckoning lights of Thames Street.

I ignored their bellows, listening only for the sounds of distance between my footfalls and theirs.

Fire tore through my back as an object made

impact. Pain ripped open my flesh and embedded in the muscle.

I stumbled, but managed to keep my feet as a scream tore from my throat, the momentum propelling my legs faster than I imagined they could go.

Dieter had thrown his knife.

And I didn't know if he had another.

Chapter Eighteen

✦✦✦

The dagger burned like hellfire in my shoulder.

Blood seeped hot into my corset and down my back, and each ragged breath felt like inhaling shards of glass. I had to get away, had to find help before Drumft and his brute caught up to finish me off.

The gas lamps wavered through the haze, mere smudges of light. Shadowy figures scurried by, averting their gazes. None dared get involved, not in this city after dark. I staggered on, praying for a miracle.

Then, by some grace, I spotted two bobbing helmets rounding the corner. The constables! I lunged for them with my last ounce of strength.

If the Ripper had done anything good for this city, it was that you couldn't stand on any corner without seeing a PC on his beat every ten minutes.

"Help me!" I cried hoarsely.

The officers rushed to me, steadying my shoulders before I collapsed. The younger one whistled sharply through his teeth at the sight of the dagger.

"You're in a bad way, miss. Get an ambulance!"

"They're. After...me," I gasped out. "They're coming!"

The constables exchanged a grave look. With a terse nod, the elder stepped in front of me while the younger kept me supported. They formed a barricade, just as Drumft's hulking silhouette appeared down the lane, the brute Dieter on his heels.

My gut twisted. I would not let them get to me again.

The officers boldly blocked their path, the elder's hand on his truncheon at his belt. The younger still supported me, though he placed his body between mine and my pursuers, a shield wrought of flesh and bone.

"Oi!" the young, fit constable called out, struck by the gravity of my desperation.

"Halt!" The elder man's voice boomed through the air, startling Drumft and Dieter into a sudden stop.

I was abandoned to lean against the stone edifice of a building as, with their batons raised and ready for action, the two officers moved against them.

Dieter, fueled by anger and adrenaline, lashed out, but the elder constable subdued him with some difficulty, catching an elbow to the trunk for his troubles.

Drumft shouted a sentence of what sounded like all

consonants, and Dieter's struggle was immediately quelled.

"Put your hands behind your back," the first constable said as he snapped cuffs onto Drumft's wrists. A look of displeasure flitted across the Prussian dignitary's face, but he complied without further resistance. The second constable followed suit, securing Dieter's hands behind him.

Drumft was still in the young officer's hold, but the purpling of his skin belied his calm. "Unhand me! I am a diplomat of the Prussian Empire. I was appointed by Otto von Bismarck himself! I'll see you both sacked for this."

The constables traded uneasy looks, but did not release him.

"Sir, you must understand." Drumft's bellow turned to a hiss as he attempted to be reasonable. "This woman attacked me unprovoked."

"An attacker, is she?" Doubt clouded the constable's gaze clear blue gaze as he glanced at his partner. "Explain how she were stabbed in the back, then."

Drumft's color went from purple to apoplectic. "An Irish Gypsy, she is. Probably had her hands in my pockets. Search her! Search her you'll find my missing gold pin!"

As I leaned against the cool brick, a wave of dizziness threatened to topple me. The world blurred at its edges, and I clutched at the wall for support. My breaths came in ragged gasps, each one a battle.

"Miss, are you all right? Can you wait for the ambulance?"

"Fine," I lied through clenched teeth, unwilling to show vulnerability even as darkness nibbled at my consciousness. "The oak leaf. Left at Lena Goldman's murder." I stabbed a damning finger in Drumft's direction, even as the lines around his form began to blur. "He confessed to killing three women."

"Not women!" Drumft roared. "*Jews!* I am an innocent man." He injected a plaintive note into his voice. "Surely you won't take the word of a deranged immigrant over a respectable gentleman like myself? Look what she's done to me!" He pointed to where the chair leg had connected with his face. Blood still dripped from his nose and a split by his cheekbone.

The younger officer frowned, glancing between us. But the elder was unmoved.

"You are both under arrest for assault and attempted murder. You can explain yourself to the magistrate." With a swift motion, he struck Drumft's uninjured cheek with his baton, sending the man reeling and blood running fresh.

"Turn the other cheek, as *your* people say," The officer spat at Drumft's feet, and that was when I saw his badge and name tag.

His name was Abraham Cohen.

WHEN I WOKE, pale daylight filtered through the hospital room windows. I shifted, then winced as pain lanced through my shoulder. The events of the previous night flooded back. Drumft's attack, my desperate flight, the police intervening just in time.

The subsequent interviews and statements and surgery to safely extract the dagger without my bleeding to death.

I was alive.

Groaning, I attempted to shift my weight and grimaced at the sharp pain. My body was a battleground of pain and medication, but it was the inability to lean back without agony that drew from me a string of curses fit for the East End docks. The doctor had said it would be several weeks before I could even think about resuming normal activity—a laughable concept, as if any part of my life had ever been normal.

The February chill intensified as a shadow fell over the doorway.

Detective Croft.

He assessed me thoroughly, his face as unreadable as stone, and was accompanied by another detective, whose presence seemed to swallow up the room's meager comfort.

Hope fluttered within my chest at the sight of him, only to be doused as quickly as it had ignited. There was no warmth in his gaze, no familiar glimmer of cama- raderie.

He was still angry, then.

"Miss Mahoney," he began, his voice carrying the detachment of duty rather than the intimacy of friendship. "This is Detective Inspector Jones. We are here as a professional courtesy to inform you..."

I held my breath, anticipating a victory, a sliver of justice in this forsaken city. But the words that spilled from Croft's lips were daggers of their own, each syllable laced with the poison of disillusionment.

"Due to a treaty of diplomatic immunity," Detective Jones intervened, "Oswald J. Drumft will not stand trial for his crimes committed on British soil."

"Immunity?" I echoed, the word tasting of ash and betrayal. "He confessed to murder."

Croft shook his head. "Our hands are tied. Drumft is returning to Berlin today. There's nothing more to be done."

"Nothing more—" A bitter laugh clawed its way out. "You tell me that a monster walks free because of some papers? Some agreement between governments?"

"Unfortunately, yes." Croft's jaw tightened.

"Then whose hands are capable enough to deliver justice?" I demanded, my voice quivering with fury and despair.

He showed me empty palms for an answer before half turning from me.

"Detective Croft," I said, my voice threaded with a plea for recognition, for any sign of the friendship we'd once cultivated amidst the mire of London's foulest crimes. But he bestowed nothing more than a curt nod, a professional boundary erected where there once stood an unspoken understanding.

Jones offered a sympathetic tilt of the head before following his superior. Their departure loomed over the room, leaving a void where warmth should reside.

Fury boiled up in me, but it was no use.

Drumft was untouchable, and Croft was closed to me. I had never felt so powerless. So there I lay, impotent in my rage, my thoughts circling like carrion birds around the carcass of what little faith I had left in the world.

Alone now, truly alone, I felt the dam holding back my emotions begin to crumble. I could no longer hold the façade of the strong, unwavering woman who delved into the darkest of humanity's sins to scrape away the remnants.

Tears welled up from a wellspring of sorrow long suppressed. They traced hot, salty paths down my cheeks, the release both a balm and a poison. I sobbed, the sound muted within the confines of my sterile prison, a lamentation for justice denied, for the lives extinguished, and for the connection with Croft—the connection we'd forged over long nights puzzling out clues and trading stories of our pasts.

We were strangers again.

The weight of everything—the hatred a man like Drumft could carry for an entire people, the brush with death, the loss of a friend through no fault but my own, and the haunting visage of an unavenged Mary Kelly—

pressed upon me with the heaviness of a shroud. Each breath became a struggle against the tide of despair, each tear a testament to the fragility of hope in a world so rife with darkness.

I cried until pain shot through my shoulder with every shallow breath. The starched hospital linens were a poor comfort, rustling like autumn leaves with each turn and toss in the narrow bed. Night had fallen once more over London, and with it, a somber stillness seeped into the ward.

Lying amidst the antiseptic scents and shadowy silhouettes of medical apparatus, I found myself adrift in thought, my consciousness threading together the tattered remnants of recent events. The visceral fear that had coursed through my veins as I fled Drumft's malevolent grasp was now transmuted into a simmering rage, fueling a determination that no blade or betrayal could diminish.

Strength wove its way through my sinews, undeterred by the wound in my back. This city had seen too many shadows dance upon its cobblestones, too many cries muffled by the thick fog that rolled off the Thames. There was *still* a devil amongst us, his signature carved into the flesh of those he took. Jack the Ripper —a name that echoed in the darkest corners of my mind, a macabre litany that would not be stilled until justice was served.

A rap at the door jolted me from my reverie, casting a sharp contrast against the solitude that had become my refuge. It was Darcy, the Dublin Destroyer, his frame filling the doorway, eyes awash with concern. He was a stalwart presence, an anchor in the tempest that had become my life. His loyalty was a balm to my weary spirit, and in the unspoken language of old friends, we shared a moment of solace.

"Ye look like hell, Fiona," he remarked, the ghost of a smile playing upon his lips.

"Ever the charmer, I see," I managed, my voice but a whisper. "But truly, it's good to find you here."

"I can't tell you how happy I am you're all right," he said, taking a seat beside me. "How grateful I am to you, not just for clearing my name, but for—for being a friend. Even after you learned certain things."

His words were a salve, a reminder that despite the treachery that danced like specters around us, there remained a constancy in our bond. There was comfort in the knowledge that Darcy stood with me, that he was glad I stood with him.

"You can rest for a bit," he said, gingerly tapping me on the good shoulder. "If you don't mind, I'll stick around a wee bit. Catch up and keep you company while you recover?"

"Rest is a luxury afforded to those without demons at their heels," I replied, my gaze never leaving the window. "Mary's ghost won't rest until I find Jack."

"Your demons can wait," Darcy huffed, adjusting my pillows with more force than necessary. "Especially that one. He'll be here. But I knew Mary to be a kind girl. She'd tell you that the living have need of you still."

His words, meant to comfort, only served to chisel away at the tomb of uncertainty I found myself ensconced within.

The living...

Darcy, his loyalty a beacon in the tempest of betrayal. Night Horse, the enigmatic lover, whose motives were as shadowy as the alleys he owned. Croft, Phillips, my household, my allies, my adversaries—the lines between them blurred like ink on damp parchment as tears threatened me once again.

I realized, as I looked over at the one person who could anchor me to my past...the living had need of me, and as much as I hated to admit it, I needed them, too.

Epilogue

A MONTH LATER...

❧❧❧

I perched upon the edge of my worn mahogany chair, the quill trembling between my fingers as I etched words onto paper—a futile endeavor to weave a tapestry of apologies without revealing too much. The ink bled into the parchment like a guilty conscience staining a pure soul. Croft and his sister deserved truth wrapped in layers of protection, not the deceit that had become my shroud. Each word was an agony, a reminder of the wrong turn taken despite my best intentions.

Dear Croft, I began, only to pause and press my lips together in frustration. How could I express the depths of my torment? That my silence was not indifference but preservation? I scratched out the words and tried anew, *My dear friends,* but it still rang hollow, false.

A gust of wind rattled the windowpane, mirroring the tempest within me. Jorah's absence loomed like a specter in the darkest corner of the room. Why had he not come after learning of my injury? Was his heart so callous, or did his silence cloak a deeper turmoil?

We might have been lovers, entwined in passion's most delicate dance, yet fate—and my own fickle heart —had severed what could have been. I wondered if whispers of my closeness with Night Horse had reached his ears, and whether jealousy or indifference painted his thoughts.

What had sparked the conflict between Jorah and Night Horse? Two titans clashing in shadows, their enmity a puzzle missing vital pieces. Could it be related to the very secrets that I kept ensconced within my chest, as heavy as the silver locket hanging from my neck?

As the candle flickered, casting dancing shadows upon the walls, my mind wove through the labyrinth of my relationships with these men—each a strand in the web of my existence, each capable of unraveling the fragile balance I maintained. With a sigh, I set the pen aside, the letter unfinished, incomplete as the emotions that besieged me.

"Perhaps tomorrow," I whispered to the empty room, my voice a ghostly echo, "clarity will come with the dawn." But even as I spoke the words, I knew that some truths were destined to remain cloaked in the fog-laden night of London, elusive as the whisper of silk against skin or the softest sigh of a broken heart.

The inkwell lay abandoned, its obsidian contents

neglected as my thoughts strayed to the echoing halls of Night Horse's residence—a mausoleum of whispered secrets and hidden desires. I had traversed there, cloaked in the audacity of daylight, only to be met with news that cleaved through my hopes like a blade.

"Mr. Night Horse has embarked on travels abroad, Miss Mahoney," the butler had intoned, his face an impassive mask belying the tumult his words conjured within me. "The duration of his absence remains...undetermined."

I pressed my lips together, tasting the bitter tincture of longing and curiosity. The chambers of my heart resounded with unanswered questions, each beat a dull thrum against the void left by his sudden departure. Night Horse, the enigma, had vanished into the mists of uncertainty, and I, bound to London's grimy cobblestones, could only wonder at his purpose.

The door creaked open, snapping me back to the stark reality of my dimly lit chamber. Darcy stood framed in the threshold, his fighter's physique incongruous against the delicate tapestry adorning the walls. Concern furrowed his brow, but his eyes held a warmth that coaxed a fragile smile from my lips.

"Ye look like ye've been wrestlin' with ghosts, Fiona," he said, crossing the room with the silent grace of a man accustomed to moving through more dangerous spaces.

"Perhaps I have," I admitted, my voice a mere wisp of sound.

"Come now," he chided gently, offering his hand, calloused yet surprisingly tender. "Tonight, we'll chase away specters with a bit of merriment. Oscar, George, and I are whiskin' ye away to the Painted Veil... They're hosting the Order of the Green Carnation tonight. Nothin' too strenuous for that shoulder of yers, I promise. Just a bit of fun," he added, holding his hands up against a forthcoming excuse.

His invitation hung in the air between us, a lifeline cast amidst the swirling currents of my inner tempest. I eyed him, the corners of my mouth quirking upward. "And how does Mr. Wilde intend to make this an early night? His penchant for revelry is well known."

Darcy chuckled. "He gave his word. And George— well, he'd carry ye home himself before lettin' the night claim ye."

"An early night," I said, skepticism lacing my tone. Yet the prospect of laughter and lightness beckoned, a siren's call drawing me from the depths.

"An early night," Darcy affirmed, his gaze steady upon mine.

"Very well," I conceded, pushing aside the missives of gloom that cluttered my desk. "Let us tempt fate and seek solace in the company of friends."

For tonight, I would don the masque of normalcy, allowing the camaraderie of dear companions to shield me from the shadows that clung with vampiric tenacity. Tomorrow's darkness would come soon enough, but for a few fleeting hours, I would bask in the glow of gaslight and friendship, defying the insistence of my own brooding soul.

The door to my chamber creaked open, and in the threshold appeared George Tunstall, his broad frame silhouetted against the dim corridor. In his arms nestled little Tegan, her cherubic face a serene contrast to the labyrinth of shadows that stretched behind them. As Tunstall stepped into the room, light danced across his visage, softening the edges of his usually stern countenance.

"Look who's eager to see her Auntie Fiona," he said, his voice betraying a tenderness seldom heard from a man of his hardened disposition.

I watched, heart swelling, as Tunstall bent forward, allowing Tegan's tiny hand to reach for me with infantile enthusiasm. His fingers, though accustomed to the clench of fists in less savory circumstances, now cradled the child with an almost sacred reverence. The sight unfurled a warmth within me, seeping through the cracks of my armored heart.

"Hello, my sweet," I whispered, brushing a kiss upon Tegan's brow. I saw in her guileless eyes the reflection of a burgeoning bond, one not wrought from blood but formed in the crucible of our shared tribulations. I felt a tranquil assurance that, should the tides of fate whisk me away, she would be cherished in hands as capable as they were gentle.

"Ye've become quite the friend to her," I remarked softly.

"Someone has to watch over the wee ones," Tunstall replied, a ghost of a smile touching his lips. "And it seems I have a knack for it."

"Indeed," I agreed, the simple truth resonating between us.

Before another word could pass, the sharp rap of knuckles upon wood echoed through the room. Mary entered with the day's post cradled in her arms. Amongst the envelopes and parcels, she bore a newspaper that seemed to command immediate attention.

"Miss Mahoney, this was delivered to your door," she intoned, extending the paper toward me like a dark omen.

"Thank you, Maryann," I said, my fingers grazing the coarse print as I took it from her hold. My eyes flitted across the front page, where bold letters heralded the ghastly end of one Herr Oswald J. Drumft. The illustrated image of the knife protruding from his back was a stark reminder of justice served cold and merciless.

A shiver of satisfaction coursed through me, undeniably macabre in its nature. Night Horse had enacted a vengeance that the law would never dispense. Though I harbored no love for the path of the vigilante, in this instance, I could not suppress the gratifying thought that there was one less demon prowling the streets of our plagued city.

"Seems justice comes in many forms," Darcy observed, his gaze lingering on the paper before returning to Tegan's innocent face. "At least Vivienne can rest in peace."

"So it does," I replied, setting aside the newspaper.

For all the darkness that pervaded our existence, we were afforded these fleeting moments of light—a child's laughter, the solace found in unlikely friendships, and the ephemeral peace of knowing that, for now, we could revel in the night.

Also by Kerrigan Byrne

A GOODE GIRLS ROMANCE

Seducing a Stranger

Courting Trouble

Dancing With Danger

Tempting Fate

Crying Wolfe

Making Merry

THE BUSINESS OF BLOOD SERIES

The Business of Blood

A Treacherous Trade

A Vocation of Violence

VICTORIAN REBELS

The Highwayman

The Hunter

The Highlander

The Duke

The Scot Beds His Wife

The Duke With the Dragon Tattoo

The Earl on the Train

Nevermore Bookstore

Brewbies

Bazaar Girls

Star-Crossed

Sirens

About the Author

Kerrigan Byrne is the USA Today Bestselling and award winning author of several novels in both the romance and mystery genre.

She lives on the Olympic Peninsula in Washington with her two Rottweiler mix rescues and one very clingy cat. When she's not writing and researching, you'll find her on the beach, kayaking, or on land eating, drinking, shopping, and attending live comedy, ballet, or too many movies.

Kerrigan loves to hear from her readers! To contact her or learn more about her books, please visit her site or find her on most social media platforms: www.kerrig anbyrne.com

Printed in the USA
CPSIA information can be obtained
at www.ICGtesting.com
LVHW040146061024
793014LV00004B/886

9 781648 395796